FROM HERE TO HEAVEN

By

Thomas Sapio

ISBN: 1-4033-0924-8 (E-book)
ISBN: 1-4033-0925-6 (Paperback)

Library of Congress Conrol Number: 2002102978

This book is printed on acid free paper.

Printed in the United States of America
Bloomington, IN

1st Books - rev. 06/28/02

April 4, 1981

When this you see
remember me.
And think of me not
unkind.
Although your face I
seldom see you are always
in my mind

Grandpa Frank

Cover photo contributed by Thomas Sapio. All information referenced in this book was told by the author's father, Frank Sapio. Nothing from this book originated from any other sources. Although some of the names may not be completely accurate, the following fictional account is based on real people, places and events.

Contents

Dedication

For Frank And Anne

And

All The Future Generations To Come

Prologue

The stories we hear as children aren't always important at the time, but they stay in our minds forever. When we are grown, these stories and the search for mysteries from the past become obsessions that come from the heart, and the way you feel about someone close to you, and how the forces of spirits from beyond can stand by you to influence and guide you. My forces are from angels that have been with me all my life. One is still on this earth physically. The other one's body is gone, but his spirit is here and has helped me make this journey into the past with him to find his mother. The mother he never knew. I invite you to come with me.

The date is September 12, 1988. The place: Madison a small picturesque town in north central New Jersey, with neatly manicured yards, and homes dating back to the time of the Revolutionary War.

In Madison everyone knows everyone else. Famous at the turn of the century for the thousands of roses grown here and shipped daily by train to New York City. The town is known to many as simply "The Rose City." In the surrounding country side, old glass greenhouses line the roads for miles and well-preserved mansions sit in aloof splendor, beyond the beautifully landscaped lawns.

Marcellus Hartley Dodge, chairman of Remington Arms, and his wife, Geraldine Rockefeller Dodge lived here. And just up the road Hamilton Twombly, son of a wealthy shipping merchant, and his wife, the former Florence Vanderbilt, lived in a 110 room mansion. Other prominent citizens were John Green, a New York City industrialist and Leslie Ward, the founder of Prudential Insurance. They all lived in and near Madison at the time.

Madison was also a magnet for Italian and Irish immigrants from the late 1800s to the early 1900s. There was plenty of work for them as groundskeepers and gardeners on these large estates. Others worked in the greenhouses as rose growers.

My father, a gentle and hard working man, grew up in Madison. He was a wonderful father and a best friend. Everyone loved Frank.

Although I no longer live in Madison, I go back when ever I can, for Madison will always be close to my heart. I can still picture my father working in the yard, but always ready to stop to talk with any old-timer who ambles by. Yet my story begins the day my father's life ended. He was 83 years old.

Chapter One

The Old Homestead

Frank hadn't been feeling good all day. He was never one to go to the doctors for every little thing. That night on September 12th, he awoke and climbed out of bed. Not wanting to wake my mother Anne, he headed quietly towards the bathroom. Halfway there feeling weak, he simply sat down on the floor with his back against the wall, and closed his eyes.

Anne awakens. Frank is not lying next to her. She gets up to check on him. Turning the corner into the hall, she switches the light on. She sees him sitting on the floor propped against the wall as if he is asleep.

She realizes that something is wrong.

"Frank," Anne yells. "What are you doing?"

He doesn't answer. She kneels beside him, gently shaking his shoulder. "Frank please get up." But he doesn't.

A tear rolls down her cheek as she looks at him. "Oh Frank please talk to me."

Unseen, Frank's spirit is still alive hovering over his own body.

He sees Anne and calls out to her. "Anne, I'm right here!"

She doesn't hear him, so she doesn't answer. Frank is confused.

Why can't she hear him? Then he realizes what has happened when he sees his body on the floor. Now all he can do is watch.

Anne rises and without looking away from Frank, she goes to the hallway phone and dials 9-1-1. Trembling, she tells the dispatcher she thinks her husband has passed away. She gives the address and reluctantly hangs up.

Numb and empty Anne walks back to Frank. Most of her life, they have been together. She doesn't know how to live without him. She just wants to sit there, next to him. The quiet of the house is painful, and only memories remain. She waits. She hears distant sirens, and realizes that this is real and not a nightmare. She cries silently for a moment.

As reality sets in, she is overwhelmed with emotions. The ambulance pulls into the driveway.

My father's spirit is still standing next to her. He embraces her helplessly. "I love you Anne, I always will."

Again, she doesn't hear him, so she doesn't answer.

The paramedics are in the hallway now, trying to revive him. But at 3:00 a.m. he is pronounced dead.

I was taking my father's death very hard, because I hadn't been there to say good-bye. Years before, just back from Vietnam, I found it difficult to accept the beliefs of my up bringing; that there was a better place after death. Like so many other veterans, I was restless, and decided to travel the country to find myself. I believe my decision to leave disappointed my mom and dad.

Eventually I settled in Texas. I married and had a family of my own. Even though my parents visited us every year, I always found their stays too brief. As they aged, it was even harder to see them go back to Madison. And now, daddy's long life had ended.

On the first day of the wake, after everyone had gone, I sat there and looked at him. I didn't want him to be left alone. The quietness of the funeral parlor was almost uneasy and left me with a sense of great sadness.

That same night, my mother got ready for bed like she did every night, she prayed. But this night she prayed for the peaceful entrance of her husband into heaven. She sat down on the edge of her bed and read prayers to the Blessed Virgin Mary. She was, and still is a devout Catholic. She is special and I give her credit for showing great strength as a woman, mother and wife.

This night was a little different than other nights. When she was done praying, she saw a figure come into her bedroom wrapped in a blanket as if it were cold. With uncertainty she looked closer and realized it was my father. He stood in complete silence looking at my mother. Then he walked to his side of the bed and sat on the edge of it. My mother didn't know what to do; she didn't know if she was dreaming or hallucinating. Before she could gather her bearings, he disappeared.

The next morning she told me what had happened. She said there was a sadness in his eyes, that she would never forget. We decided that he didn't want to leave this world yet. That thought lingered in my mind. Something must be keeping him here, but what?

The funeral was planned at Saint Vincent's Church, which was the first and only Catholic Church in Madison. Both of my parents had attended Saint Vincent's since they were children.

The funeral mass was impressive and over a hundred people attended. My father was greatly loved. The priest spoke of his kindness towards others, his love for Anne and all of his family.

After the funeral mass, the family and I decided that the procession should take my father past his old homestead one last time.

It was right across the street from where my parents lived, and where he passed away. The hearse carrying my father stopped in front momentarily.

His favorite room in the house was the TV room where he would relax in his lounge chair. He would frequently get up and look out the window and see his old homestead. He loved the sight of the old house.

There was a peacefulness about this house. Built in 1818, it was a charming little red farmhouse with white shudders and a small front porch. It was the oldest house on the street. Characteristic of the area a short stone wall in front separated the house from the street.

He loved to talk and reminisce about the old days. I remember so many stories about his childhood. These stories have enlightened my life.

The procession continued on to the cemetery. It was a short ceremony. I didn't want it to end, because then I would have to leave him alone again. The thought of leaving him alone made me uneasy. The only reason I decided to leave the cemetery after the funeral was knowing that maybe, he would not be so lonely because there were so many of my parents' friends and relatives buried around him. Both my mother and father would joke that they chose their plot because they were close to the water faucet and parking lot. They always said, if one died before the other, the one left would not have far to carry the sprinkling pail to water the flowers, and close to the parking lot so it would make it easier for people to visit them. My parents believed that it was very important that we visit the cemetery, especially on all the holidays, when we take time to clean our loved-ones grave and leave fresh flowers or a plant. They said it wasn't proper to forget someone after they were gone, and they never forgot anyone.

We left the cemetery, and everyone went to my mother's house. The living room was crowded with people, yet I felt like something was missing. I went into their TV room and saw my father's empty lounge chair. This sight brought tears to my eyes. I walked over to the window and looked at the old homestead across the street. I had looked out this window so many times before, but for some reason it didn't feel the same.

As I stood there, I felt a strange presence of another next to me. All the voices from the living room and kitchen faded away. Before I knew it, I saw my father standing next to me peering out the window.

He turned to me and lovingly smiled. All of a sudden his smile turned to a look of sadness.

In a desperate tone he said, "Please help me Tommy. You are the only one who can."

"What do you want me to do? How can I...?"

He interrupted and said, "My mother."

I turned away to look out the window to ponder those two words. I turned back to ask what this meant, but he was no longer there. The voices from the living room suddenly bring me back to reality. I remained in that spot unable to move. I was shocked at what I had just seen. Did I imagine it? Quietly, my mother came back into the room and stood next to me. We silently peered out the window for a few minutes.

Breaking the silence she said, "Why don't you come back into the living room Tommy? Everyone is wondering where you are."

"Ma your not going to believe this, but I just saw daddy. He needs my help."

"I know," she calmly said. There was no doubt in her words.

After a moment, I realized what he meant. We had always known that he was taken from a New York City orphanage as a baby, and how he wished he had known his birth mother. He talked about it all the time.

He would not be at peace until he knew who his birth mother was.

A few weeks passed and fall was moving in. My wife and daughters had gone back to Texas without me. With each passing day those towering maple trees that surrounded the house slowly turned to a deep red and the leaves began to gently float to the ground. I kept a vigil in the TV room. I didn't want to miss seeing my father again.

I couldn't accept that he was dead. He was so much a part of everyone's lives, especially mine.

Everyday I would close my eyes and imagine the day I saw my father. I would pray to see him again, but I never did.

Another month went by and I realized that I needed to go back to Texas. I had family waiting for me there. The guilt of leaving my mother was overwhelming. She never showed her loneliness, but I knew it was there. I reassured her that I would be back soon.

As I waved good-bye from the car, I could see her eyes well up with tears. She stood at daddy's usual spot and peered out the window at me. I wanted to be strong, so I held my emotions back until I got onto the highway.

A few months went by, I started seeing my father more and more. I thought I was dreaming, but it seemed so real. He kept asking me to help him. I didn't understand what he wanted me to do. I felt compelled to delve into his past.

Again, the whole family had known that he had been taken from a New York City orphanage, and through his lifetime wondered about his birth mother. But no one seemed to know much more than I did. Using the library as a starting point, I pored over old census records and city directories. With each passing day my research became an obsession.

I obtained copies of the 1900, 1905, and 1910 state and federal census. I set up a make shift office in my bedroom at home and arranged piles of records in chronological order. My wife thought I was cracking up, but I wanted to understand the dreams I was having, my father's apparitions. I studied the records for hours at a time.

Chapter Two

Walking With Spirits

One summer night in 1989, I went to bed early. Around 10:30 I woke up to the violent sound of a tree branch slamming against the bedroom window. I quietly got out of bed and went outside to see what was going on. I opened the door to a great gust of wind. Though it was a warm night, the wind had a chill in it. Scared, I closed the door and stood there trying to gather myself. The only sound I heard was the settling of the house. I started back to my bedroom.

When all of a sudden I heard, "Tommy!"

"It was daddy's voice!"

As fast as the chill entered the room, the warmth returned with the sound of his voice. I looked over and saw my father sitting in his favorite chair, in my TV room.

"I'm so glad you came back daddy."

"I'm here for just a little while. Please help me find my mother. She is lost."

Tears ran down his face. He was gripping something in his hand that he kept looking at. Opening his hand, he revealed an old Indian head penny. Lovingly, daddy placed the penny in my open palm. His hand was warm. This, I knew, was not a dream.

He said, "When you carry this penny, you will walk with the spirits from my past. You will be able to find out who my birth mother was. Remember, carry this with you everywhere you go."

Again, before I could say anything, he disappeared.

Growing up, I loved to collect pennies. My father and I would spend hours talking about my prized collection.

#

Inspecting the penny, I suddenly feel as if I'm falling. The colors in the wallpaper and carpet blur; my house disappears. I no longer exist in the present. I look at myself. I'm dressed in formal wear not the pajamas I was wearing. My clothes are distinctly from a another time. I look around and I'm no longer in Texas, but in Madison.

I find myself in a cornfield where my mother's house should be. Trying to make sense of all this, I look at the penny still clutched in my hand. Now it looks newly minted, a moment ago it was old and worn. My confusion increases at the sight of daddy's old homestead; it faces a dirt road, not the busy street I knew. A horse and buggy stand in front of the bright red house. It's a peaceful place. Chickens mill around in the road; a milk cow grazes on the grass. The backyard is neatly manicured with fruit trees and grape arbors that seem to go on forever.

A small boy in the yard plays by himself. A rugged-looking man carries a double-barreled shotgun in one hand, and a dead raccoon in the other. He walks along the dirt road, with his hunting jacket pockets full of dead squirrels. The belted rope around his waist holds a dead pheasant. He's a tough-looking husky fellow, about six feet tall with a ruddy complexion. I recognize him as Vincenzo Sapio, my father's father. Remembering what daddy said, I assume the little boy is my father Frank. I watch as

Vincenzo approaches. Frank runs to him eager to help. Vincenzo hands him a squirrel to carry and Frank proudly walks by his side. I feel so good to be here. It looks just like daddy said it did. The air is crisp and clear in this beautiful place.

I try to get their attention but soon realize I'm invisible to them. I am only an observer. I walk to the backyard looking for my father's mother Antonetta. Turning the corner I see her. She's wearing a light colored dress, her hair is pulled back under a kerchief. She is picking vegetables and putting them in her apron. When it's full, she gathers the ends of the apron and goes towards the house. I start to follow her inside, but I'm suddenly knocked to the ground.

#

Within seconds I start seeing other visions. Before I know it I'm transported in time to which seems to be around 1900 when Vincenzo was a young man in Italy. Vincenzo was born in 1881 in Marigliano Italy, which is just outside Naples.

Marigliano is a pretty town, surrounded by rolling hills that are covered with olive orchards and grape vineyards. Every house has a garden. By the looks of things it seems to be summer. His parents are Antonio and Rosa. Vincenzo is the oldest of three brothers. The family are peasant farmers who make their living by selling vegetables.

Vincenzo works at a near-by olive orchard and helps at home. It's evident that Vincenzo's father is a hard worker, but he has a mean streak. Everyone in town is afraid of him and he is afraid of no one.

He seems to have a reputation for fighting. He is especially abusive to Vincenzo. Because he is the oldest, it is he who gets blamed when his younger brothers act up.

From morning till night the family works hard farming with little time for pleasure. What little money Vincenzo makes working at the olive orchard, Antonio demands. Antonio has no kind words or greetings for anyone. When Vincenzo comes home there is no hello from his father, only a gruff, "Where were you today, you God dam bum?"

Vincenzo doesn't answer. He lays the money on the table and walks away.

Antonio takes the money complaining that it's not enough.

Day in and day out nothing changes. For such a pretty place, it's miserable for Vincenzo.

Vincenzo's mother Rosa, is a quiet fearful woman. She never dares to interfere in the frequent altercations between Vincenzo and Antonio.

When she is not working in the garden or the vineyards, Rosa is in the kitchen cooking. She knows the routine. When Antonio comes in, his food and wine are to be on the table waiting for him. His speech is as abusive to Rosa as it is to Vincenzo. His answer to most everything Rosa says is, "Shut up you dumb mule!"

I think Antonio is a little crazy. Vincenzo doesn't like the way Antonio treats his mother. Several times I see him stand up to his father.

Today is payday for Vincenzo, and Antonio knows it. When Vincenzo walks into the kitchen, Antonio is eating supper. Without looking up from the table and with a mouth full of food he mutters, "Where's my money, you God damm bum!"

Vincenzo throws the money on the table. "You're the bum and I'm getting tired of the way you talk to ma."

Antonio says, "Keep your mouth shut, and I want more money.

You're not going to live here for nothing. I know you have more money."

Vincenzo answers, "Yeah, I do, but you're not getting it. I need something for myself. For years I have been doing what you want. You're never happy with anything. I've been giving you all my money. What have you been doing with it? I'm not going to take this anymore and I'm not going to let you holler at ma the way you do. She works hard and she deserves better."

With that, Vincenzo silently leaves the house.

Antonio yells, "Don't you walk away while I'm talking to you, God damm it!"

Vincenzo ignoring him, walks out to the barn.

Antonio follows. With his back turned towards Antonio, Vincenzo hears him say, "Don't you ever talk back to me again."

Turning, Vincenzo sees Antonio pick up a three pronged long handled hayfork near the barn door. As the hayfork comes at Vincenzo, he moves to the side. The fork catches his little finger.

Without saying anything Antonio walks back to finish his supper.

Vincenzo has had enough. He hears about some people around Marigliano who have immigrated to America. They've settled in Madison, a small town in the state of New Jersey. There is nothing to keep him here in Italy. He knows he can find work in America.

On Sunday mornings Rosa goes to mass alone. This particular Sunday, Vincenzo comes into the church before mass. He sits beside Rosa watching her as she prays. He clutches her hand and looks at her. She is crying silently. He stays beside her until mass is over.

After the mass, he says, "I've decided to leave this place mama and go to America, I'll find work there. I just can't stay here anymore, and I want you to come with me mama."

Rosa interrupts. "Vincenzo, my place is here. You go and start a new life, I'll pray for you. I know things will be better for you there. I have heard good things about America. I will be all right."

Deep in her heart, Rosa knows that she may never see her son again.

That afternoon without telling anyone, Vincenzo packs his bag and with fifty dollars in his pocket he goes to the docks where all the immigrants are waiting to board ships bound for New York City. I watch him get on the boat. I can sense that he is thinking about his mother. He is afraid he will never see her again. Sadly enough, his father probably doesn't care that he is gone. He will only miss his earnings. He feels guilty for leaving his mother, but she is an old fashion Italian woman and given the era that I am in, women stayed with their husbands no matter what. She knows that Vincenzo needs to get away for his own well-being.

The trip to New York City is anything but pleasant. Many days on an overcrowded boat, people are sea sick, and the conditions are brutal. Vincenzo doesn't care because anything would be better than where he was, and he knows that he can do better in America.

As soon as the ship passes the Statue of Liberty, I can see it in his eyes: his life has begun anew. He still has to go through the toughest part. He will need to get through the customs process at Ellis Island. Vincenzo waits apprehensively. People get turned away for one reason or another. To get through customs he knows you cannot have any medical problems and you need to have a specific destination and names of people who are expecting you. He plans to tell customs he is meeting a brother in Madison, New Jersey. Of course, there is no brother.

Luckily Vincenzo's plan works and he makes it through customs.

For a small fee he catches a ride from an Italian man by the name of Frank Viorio. Frank offers rides to Italian immigrants going to Madison. He also helps them find jobs, places to live, and later helps some of them become citizens.

Frank takes Vincenzo to get a room in a small boarding house on Elm Street, one of the very early Italian sections of Madison which encompassed North, South, East and West Streets. Before the Italians, the Irish occupied these areas.

Frank tells Vincenzo, "There is a lot of work in this town, what did you do on the other side?" The other side meaning Italy.

Vincenzo says, "I worked in the olive orchards and grape vineyards and grew vegetables. I can prune and graft fruit trees, but I will take any kind of work."

Not long after Vincenzo arrives in Madison, the area is hit with a rainstorm. It rains for two days straight. Everything is flooded including The Hillside Cemetery, one of the oldest cemeteries in Madison, with graves going back to the 18th century. Hundreds of bodies are lifted to the surface and wash down the Spring Garden Brook, which eventually flows into the Passaic River, as far as a mile away from the cemetery. Vincenzo is one of the workers who helps gather the bones to take them back to the cemetery. It is a gruesome sight. Some whole coffins float down the river smashing into trees and breaking apart.

Watching them search for remains, I remember walking through these very woods as a boy. A friend and I were checking our traps and came across something sticking out of the shallow part of the brook.

Picking it up we realized it was a bone with three teeth. Later that day I showed my father. He said it was a person's lower jawbone. That's when daddy told me about the flood and how his father Vincenzo, helped scour the woods for remains. Vincenzo thought that part of the woods was haunted. Well, our find made the front page of the local newspaper.

"Human Jawbone Poses Exciting Mystery." No one really ever knew exactly where the bone came from, although the newspaper did confirm that there was the flood, but beyond that it was never pursued. They just figured it came from the flood. My boyish imagination went crazy with this thought. From that day forward, whenever I entered that part of the woods, I felt a strange cold feeling.

Now here I was, witnessing the actual flood I'd so often heard about. I clung to my penny. I didn't want this to end. A year goes by. A brother, Feligia from Italy, joins Vincenzo and more and more families are immigrating from Italy to Madison. Most are from the small villages around Naples.

Everyone seems to know one another from the other side. Vincenzo never asks about his father. He has a new life in Madison. But he wonders about his mother and what was going on in her life. He works as a gardener on several different estates around Madison and saves his money.

A family from Marigliano moves in next door to Vincenzo. They have a daughter named Antonetta. Vincenzo sees her everyday walking to the railroad tracks to collect coal for the stove. Because he knew the family in Italy, he visits often. He and Antonetta get along well.

On March 5th, 1905, Vincenzo and Antonetta are married by Father McDowell at Saint Vincent's Church in Madison. In 1905, Saint Vincent's is a small country church on Ridgedale Avenue, with a cemetery located in back of the church and a schoolroom in the basement. It is the first Catholic Church and cemetery in Madison. It was built in 1839, but by 1905, more Catholic Irish and Italians are moving to Madison and the church is fast becoming too small. So a new beautiful Gothic style church is built in a new location. The old church steeple is torn down and the church is turned into a house. The cemetery is moved to a new location. Workers dig up and move what bodies they can find to the new cemetery. Watching them dismantle the steeple, I already know what its future holds. One family is to stay in the house until the late 1990s.

When it goes up for sale, my nephew and his wife become interested in its history. They buy it and restore it as it looked in 1906.

As for Vincenzo and Antonetta, they work hard and save enough money to move from Elm

Street to a place daddy would call his old homestead.

#

In what seems to be no time at all, I find myself back at the old homestead before my father's time.

Chapter Three

A Foundling Home

Vincenzo and Antonetta are sitting quietly at their kitchen table, I feel they are lonely. I know something is missing, my father.

I know that I am in a different time, but I don't know when. I just know that my father Frank is not with them. The whole experience is draining me, but I don't want to leave. I need to find out about daddy's biological mother. I sense that Vincenzo and Antonetta desperately want children. Antonetta is kind and loving. I know that she would make a wonderful mother, but they learn that Antonetta cannot conceive. A woman by the name of Mary Desmond befriended Antonetta when she and Vincenzo moved to the old homestead. Antonetta would visit Mary and bring her fresh vegetables from the garden occasionally.

During a visit, Antonetta says, "My husband and I want to have a family, but I've found out I can't have children. Vincenzo has been very quiet lately. I know this is bothering him, but I don't know what to do."

"Antonetta, have you and Vincenzo ever thought about adopting?" Mary asked.

"We talked about it a little, but we don't know where to go."

"I think I can help you, let me talk to Father McDowell at the church. He knows a lot of people."

When Antonetta gets home, Vincenzo is working outside adding a hayloft to the barn.

He calls out, "I need more nails up here."

Antonetta gets him a bag of nails, "I just talked to Mary, she thinks maybe we can talk to the priest about adopting a child."

Vincenzo doesn't answer, instead he takes a nail from between his teeth and continues hammering.

"Hand me that board over there," he says.

Vincenzo is not one for small talk. She continues to help and tells Vincenzo, "Mary says, Father McDowell knows a lot of people.

Maybe he can help us Vincenzo."

I can see he is taking all this in. Finally he takes the last nail out of his mouth. "Hold the ladder, I'm coming down. Let's go sit under the apple tree."

They sit silently for a moment, then Vincenzo reaches down for the jug of red wine that sits next to his bench. As he pours it, he asks, "When can we talk to the priest?"

"I'll ask Mary tomorrow. She can arrange it for us," Antonetta replies.

Early the next morning Antonetta is at Mary's house. Vincenzo wants to do it! Together, the three go meet with the priest. They talk to him about their situation. He recommends that they go to an orphanage in New York City. This particular orphanage, a foundling home is run by the Sisters of Charity. From what I can gather it seems that Saint Vincent's has a close tie to this place and there are a lot of children who need homes.

Hopeful, Vincenzo and Antonetta go home to discuss it privately.

They decide they want to pay the foundling a visit. Vincenzo wants a boy because he wants his name to be carried on after he dies.

After a week of thinking about it, they go back to tell the priest they are ready. Because Vincenzo and Antonetta speak mostly Italian, the priest asks Mary to go with them into New York City. Mary is happy to help her friend in any way that she can. The three of them leave for the city carrying a letter signed by the priest.

An attractive five-story red and white brick building on 68th Street, the foundling home is one of the largest adoption agencies in the United States. Children are left here for so many different reasons. The huge influx of immigrants during this time makes housing and poverty a big problem. Often children are simply abandoned and found in the streets by strangers or a policeman, perhaps abandoned by an unwed mother, or a mother with an abusive or alcoholic husband.

While others are left on the doorstep of the foundling in the middle of the night wrapped in a blanket with a note, and found the next morning by a sister. If a mother has the courage to take her baby inside, the baby is placed in a basket in the reception room, where the sister asks the child's name and date of birth. Most likely the child will never see his or her parent again. Some of the children are put on trains and shipped out west to be placed with families wanting children. Sadly, many of these children are abused by their foster parents and often forced into a life of hard labor on their farms. Luckily the majority are placed with good families and grow up to have good lives.

I try to imagine my father's mother and why she could not keep him, but I can't. I wonder if I ever will.

It is late in the morning on Monday, July 27th, 1908. Vincenzo, Antonetta and Mary open the doors to the foundling and walk along an empty hallway. Vincenzo wears the only suit he owns. Having just pulled it out of his trunk, it still holds its wrinkles. Antonetta has her hair up in a bun. she is wearing a long, plain brown dress, and a gold chain with a crucifix around her neck. In contrast, Mary is very well dressed. She wears a dark suit with a high-necked white ruffled blouse.

As they walk down the hallway, they are met by one of the sisters that proceeds to lead them to Sister Vincent at the front desk. Mary introduces herself, Vincenzo, and Antonetta. She hands the letter from Father McDowell to the sister. She takes a few minutes to read it over.

After their preliminary discussions with the sister, they are led up several flights of stairs to a large room lined with cribs. Babies of all sizes wait for someone to adopt them. In another room, the older children gather to play games. They do not want an older child. I feel I know Vincenzo by now. I know he wants a young boy so he can teach him his ways, and he doesn't want a child that will remember where he came from. A sister tells them to look around. If they see a baby that they want, take the name tag from the child's crib back to the front desk so they can begin to start the paper work.

They continue to walk and look. There are so many children to choose from. There is one baby that captures Vincenzo and Antonetta's attention. A thin, sweet looking little boy with blond hair and piercing blue eyes, which seem to have a twinkle in them. He appears to be about three years old. All the cribs have name tags. Because neither Vincenzo or Antonetta can read English, Mary tells them the baby's name is Edwin. With his stern weather-worn face, Vincenzo peers down at Edwin. Without hesitation Edwin innocently smiles at him. But Vincenzo does not give in to the baby's charm. He does not smile back. The couple continue to look at the other babies, but for some reason Vincenzo is drawn to keep looking back at Edwin. Every time Vincenzo looks back at the baby, Edwin smiles and reaches out for him. Finally, Vincenzo walks back to Edwin and Edwin pulls gently on Vincenzo's sleeve.

Vincenzo looks down and in broken English says, "How come nobody took you from here boy?"

Antonetta hears Vincenzo's voice and walks over. She picks Edwin up out of his crib. Edwin puts his arms around her and lays his head on her shoulder as if to say, "Please take me."

Vincenzo looks at Antonetta and says, "He's skinny but we will fatten him up."

Antonetta tells Vincenzo, "He will be a good boy and he can carry on our name Vincenzo."

It is an easy choice. Antonetta gently places Edwin back down in his crib and walks back to the main desk with Mary and Vincenzo. Mary tells Sister Vincent that Mr. and Mrs. Sapio are interested in the baby Edwin.

The sister says, "You made a good choice, Edwin is one of our best children. Edwin will turn three years old soon, he was born on October 12th, 1905. He has been with us since he was an infant. He came to us in the morning hours when he was just about a month old because his mother was not able to keep him. When his mother left him with us he had already been baptized. If you want to take Edwin, we do have a policy that a nurse visit your home every so often to check on the boy and the living conditions until he turns twenty-one."

They continue to talk and Mary helps fill out the necessary paper work.

While they are doing that, I walk back to Edwin's crib. I look at him and he looks at me with those piercing blue eyes as though for those few seconds, I am visible to him, and he is saying thank you. He reaches out for my hand, I take it and smile back at him. I am so astonished at what is happening!

I begin talking to him. "Do you know who I am? I'm Tommy, I am so happy for you. You will be happy...."

I'm interrupted with the sound of a sister's voice. "Come on Edwin I'm going to dress you real nice. We've found a good home for you."

I know he saw me today and that we made eye contact.

The sister picks him up and hugs him. "We will miss you Edwin, you're such a good boy."

I walk back to the front desk. Vincenzo, Antonetta and Mary are just finishing all the paper work. The sister takes them to a parlor where they sit and wait. Within a few minutes Edwin is brought in. His hair is combed neatly to the right and he is wearing a white dress, which looks like a baby doll dress, with black tights and black pointed lace-up shoes, that extend just above the ankle.

So this beautiful summer day in 1908, is to be Edwin's last day at the foundling. Sadly, he used to watch so many people come and go with babies, but never got chosen. Even though he is only three years old he seems to understand what is going on and he is happy that he has finally found a real home.

His new parents take him home to Madison. His name is to be Frank. They name him after Frank who helped Vincenzo when he first got off the boat at Ellis Island. Vincenzo's brother Feligia is waiting, and he thinks it's a good idea that the men have their picture taken together. I don't think that women are highly thought of during this time, because they did not include Antonetta in the photo. In fact they didn't even ask her if she wanted to go with them. They just went and did it without telling her. She didn't seem to care anyway, she just accepted whatever Vincenzo decided to do. They raise Frank as though he is their own. I can tell how proud they are of their new son. Vincenzo and Antonetta take him everywhere and show him everything. But they are especially proud of the homestead. Picking him up, they show him all that they have done in the short time that they have lived here. Frank is especially amused with all the farm animals which he had never seen.

Every animal has a name, with the exception of the chickens because there are far too many and they all look alike.

Vincenzo and Antonetta speak very broken with a very heavy Italian accent. Half of what they say in one sentence is Italian and the other half English. It is almost comical to watch and hear them trying to describe things to Frank. Frank is used to what the nuns had taught him at the foundling. This is all new to him but he listens intently and somehow picks up on what they are saying. Vincenzo's voice is rough and raspy sounding. While Antonetta's is sweet, and she smiles and laughs a lot. She is a very kind and loving person who tries to please everyone. I can see that Frank is content. Because Vincenzo needs help, Frank is learning how to work at a very young age. Vincenzo is a tough man and as strong as an ox. He is a man of very few words.

He seems as though he doesn't trust too many people. When gypsy peddlers come around, he runs them off. He is very protective of his family, this is all that he cares about. He seems to be hardened by his tough up bringing and the way his father treated him. But unlike his father, he is good to his son Frank. Vincenzo doesn't make a whole lot of money, but he saves when he can. Finally, he is able to save enough money to buy a little over an acre of land directly across the street from the old homestead. This eventually will become the place where my mother and father will build their home.

It is late fall and after working long hours, Vincenzo diligently continues to work at night clearing his new land that he is so proud of. He hooks Blacky the old workhorse up and tills the ground to create their own cornfield. Frank follows close behind his father. In trying to keep up with him and the old workhorse he falls in the furrows. He gets up without saying a word and runs to catch up. By spring the ground is warm enough to plant. They sell some of the corn, but they keep most of it for themselves.

Vincenzo invests in another piece of property just down the street from the old homestead. There's about three acres with a farmhouse that dates back to 1850. It's a pretty, white, two-story home, with lapped siding and a front porch. The trim appears to be hand made. As I look closer the gutters are wood and built right into the house like a work of art. The cellar is deep with stone walls. Tree trunks act as beams that hold the upper floors. It needs some work but overall it's in pretty good shape. Vincenzo doesn't waste any time. He paints it, rents it out and begins to add on to the back to make it into a two family home. Frank follows him everywhere and watches closely. They work from sun up to sun down. I wonder how they get so much accomplished in such a short time. There is room on the side of the property and they plant more corn.

Back at the old homestead Antonetta takes care of the farm animals and tends to the garden. Supper is always on the table when they get home. It is amazing to see my father as a boy growing up and seeing the old homestead as it looked back then with the gardens and all the young fruit trees that are bearing fruit.

Around 1910, Feligia decides to go back to Italy. He misses the old country and Vincenzo is busy with his own family. Feligia is different than Vincenzo. He likes fine clothes and doesn't believe in all this hard work. He thinks that there are easier ways to make money.

What's weird about it, he never seems to work but he always has rolls of money. He likes to give Frank money, but Vincenzo doesn't like handouts and he wants Frank to learn the value of money.

I don't know what Feligia does. He never tells anyone. I think he might have something going on in the city. I just know that no one sees him for along time, then he is back again. Then one day he says good-bye to Vincenzo and never comes back.

Once or twice a year a woman from the foundling would stop by and talk to Vincenzo and Antonetta. Although Frank sees her, they never tell him who she is. He just thinks that she is a friend of the family.

They never mention the foundling and never say anything to him about where he came from. Frank always thought that he was born right here in the old homestead.

Vincenzo decides that Frank is old enough to go to school. Just down the street about halfway between the old homestead and the 1850 farmhouse is an old, one room-red brick schoolhouse. Vincenzo tells him that this is where he will go to school. It's close enough to the house that he is able to walk and when he learns how, he can ride his bicycle. Frank is intimidated by this big responsibility, but he wants to make his father proud. So he reluctantly agrees.

Chapter Four

A Beloved Friend

Frank begins school, but because he is the youngest in the class, it's hard for him to make friends. He doesn't want to say anything to his parents; he's afraid that they will be disappointed in him. It's evident to Antonetta and Vincenzo that he is having a difficult time.

To Frank's surprise, they transfer him to Saint Vincent's. It's no more than a mile from home. There's about thirty children in the whole school. Most of the children's parents are Italian and Irish immigrants. Frank loves it immediately because the children are more his own age. He begins riding his bicycle to school.

I had always heard stories about all the dogs they had and that most of them slept in every room in the house, and how they would hang around the kitchen table looking for scraps that fell to the floor. At this particular time I count ten. They love Frank and since most of them were around when Frank first came here, they are his friends. Some would follow him to school, while others follow Vincenzo when he hunts.

I watch Frank as he plays with the dogs, one of which I remember from stories I had heard, and old photographs—I'd seen of his beloved fox terrier named Bocce. He was a puppy when Vincenzo brought him home for Frank a few years before. He is truly a special friend. He follows Frank everywhere. Bocce loves riding in the basket on the front of his bicycle. I can tell that the dog has the same affection for my father as my father has for him. I remember my father telling me they named him Bocce because when the men played bocce ball, he would run up and down the sidelines like some kind of referee. But for some reason he would never touch the balls. I watch as Bocce rides to school everyday in the basket. The wind blowing in his face, he looks so proud to be with Frank.

When they arrive at school it's early. Frank is always early. He sits on the ground outside the window of the classroom, Bocce sits on his lap and keeps staring at him.

Frank says, "I want you to come in with me, but I will get in trouble. Sister Hildagar won't let you come in. I'll be right inside this window so we can see each other."

Bocce knows the routine as they go through this everyday.

Frank walks inside and Bocce doesn't take his eyes off of the window.

When he sees Frank he curls up in a little ball, closes his eyes, and dozes off. Every now and then he awakens to make sure Frank is still there. At recess the kids play outside, Bocce watches in excitement. At lunch, Frank sits outside the window with some of the other kids and shares his lunch with Bocce. Then towards the end of the day, Bocce barks outside the window, as if he is telling Frank he is tired of waiting.

Frank looks and says, "Shhh your going to get me in trouble."

Sister Hildagar goes outside to scold the dog. She claps her hands, waves her finger and tries to chase him, but Bocce talks back to her.

"You stop that right now young man," she yells.

The children in the class giggle when they look out the window and see Bocce barking at the sister. Bocce runs a few feet away, only to come right back, laying down with his head between his front paws giving her this innocent look. The sister cracks a smile at Bocce, hoping the kids do not see her. The kids run back to their seats before she comes back in to resume class. After school Frank and his trusty friend head home.

On their way, they pass through Madison. Everyone in town knows Frank and Bocce. All the store owners and old timers wave as they ride by on Frank's bicycle. With only four or five houses between the homestead and Madison, they make there way home. It is a narrow dirt road that Frank takes everyday. Like every town there are bullies. One day between school and home, a group of older kids see Frank and Bocce coming home. They block the narrow road so they can't get through. They have no choice but to stop. Bocce senses that they are up to no good.

He looks at Frank then looks at them and shows his teeth. They begin to tease and push Frank, Bocce barks from his basket.

The bully leader asks Frank, "Where are you going sissy, home with your wop mommy and daddy?"

These kids aren't Italian or else they wouldn't be calling Vincenzo and Antonetta wops, and evidentially they don't know Vincenzo very well. The man of few words was no one to get cross with, especially when it comes to his family. Frank doesn't want to fight, he just wants to get home to help his parents. They keep on. Finally Frank has no choice, he fights back. The leader is older and bigger than Frank. I never imagined that Frank had it in him, and where he learned how is beyond me, but he can really fight. I think these kids are sorry that they started this mess and on top of everything, Bocce makes a flying leap out of his basket and violently starts tearing at the bully's ankle. He bites him pretty good and the boy falls to the ground. Bocce turns to the others and shows his teeth. They run away and he chases them. Frank was actually doing pretty good without him, but I think Bocce wanted a piece of the action.

The beaten bully says, "Okay, okay I've had enough!"

Frank never said anything during this altercation.

He lets the boy up and then tells him, "Don't you ever call my mother and father a name again."

The boy walks away nearly in tears. Bocce shakes off. Frank bends down and picks him up. Bocce licks him in the face. Frank has a black eye, but he doesn't know it until he gets home and Antonetta sees it.

When they get home Bocce goes to his spot and lays down.

Antonetta sees Frank. Startled, she asks, "Oh mama mia Frank!

What happened?"

He tells her the story and says that he doesn't think that those boys will bother him again.

Antonetta feels bad about what happened and is worried about what Vincenzo will do when he comes home. Just then he walks in. He looks at Frank and says, "Did you get the best of him Frank?"

Frank tells his parents why the fight started and Vincenzo tells him, "A lot of people don't like the Italians and the colored people.

They call us wops and they call the colored people niggers. Maybe someday things will be different, but I will probably be dead by the time that happens."

As they sit and talk, someone knocks on the door. Antonetta goes to the door and standing there, is the beat up looking boy with his father.

He begins telling Antonetta, "Look what your son did to my boy. I want an apology....."

Interrupting, Vincenzo yells, "Who's there?" He walks to the door and in his usual rough voice tells Antonetta, "Go back into the kitchen I'll take care of this."

Bocce knows who it is and begins barking. Vincenzo tells him to go lay down and Bocce obeys.

He reaches for his twelve-gauge double-barreled shotgun and tells the man, "Here's my apology, If you, your son or any of his friends ever bother my boy again, or if you come to my door or even walk by my house, this is what you'll get!"

He grabs the man by the front of his shirt with one hand pushing him backwards, and with the other hand he raises the shotgun, showing it to the man, explaining, "I don't want to see you walk down the same side of the street as me or my boy, and if I am in town in the same store as you, I want you to leave, so I don't have to look at your face!"

He knocks the man to the ground and says, "Do you understand what I'm telling you? Now get off my property!"

The man leaves without incident. Vincenzo, the man of few words, would scare anyone.

They put in a hard day today. Bocce is worn out. He and Frank sleep good tonight.

Frank never saw those boys on his street again. And if he did see them in town, Bocce would growl and show his teeth. It seemed as though their little gang broke up after that incident and as far as the boy's father, he did exactly what Vincenzo told him to do, and as long as he did, he would never have any trouble from Vincenzo.

The winters are long and harsh, Vincenzo takes Frank hunting as much as possible and shows him the secrets of the woods. Frank loves the time spent with his father and looks forward to their adventures.

Fur coats are becoming popular. So on weekends when Frank is not in school, they take up trapping. Muskrat and mink is where the money is.

It isn't unusual to get one dollar for a good muskrat pelt skinned and stretched. Mink on the other hand are five dollars or more per pelt, if you are smart enough to catch one. If there is even the slightest scent of a human, the mink will not get near. But somehow Vincenzo and Frank are cunning enough to outsmart at least one or two. Because they are a little bit harder to catch, they concentrate mostly on muskrats.

Walking along the Spring Garden and down to the Passaic River, they expertly know all the animals' tracks, where they hide, sleep and eat, setting at least fifty traps. Because these animals move mostly at night, they begin their journey just after lunch on Saturday afternoon not getting back until night-fall. If the snow is to deep, Bocce stays home with Antonetta. But most of the time he goes, he doesn't want to miss a trick. The next morning they are up at 4:30 to do what needs to be done with the farm animals. They eat a hearty breakfast that Antonetta prepares, and about thirty minutes before it begins to get light, they make their way towards the woods to collect their catch.

Vincenzo carries a shot-gun no matter where he goes, sometimes walking up on a stray pheasant. I watch, as some of the spots in the water where the traps are set, are frozen. I shiver as Vincenzo breaks the ice and sticks his arm in the icy water to pull out a frozen muskrat.

Out of fifty *traps* they catch at least forty muskrats and one mink.

They did very well today. They collect the furs and traps putting them in burlap bags and head home. It's all they can do to carry them home.

They do this during the winter months on weekends, putting them on stretchers and storing them in the barn until late winter or early spring, then selling the pelts to the local fur dealer. At this rate depending on how many traps they set, they could accumulate about five to eight hundred pelts by the end of winter. It took them a better part of the day today. Vincenzo sits at the kitchen table and reaches for his jug of red wine. This warms him up. It seems cruel to trap these poor animals, but this is a way of life, and they need to make a living somehow.

Time moves on and Frank is in the fifth grade now. Sister Margaret Mary is the teacher for this year. He begins to find time after school to set a few of his own traps. Getting up early enough to check them before school. Bocce is at his side almost always and if he doesn't ride his bicycle with Bocce in the basket, they walk together. Frank carries a blanket for Bocce on real cold days and sets it up outside the window at the school, under the overhang. Some of the sisters feel sorry for him outside in the snow and let him in, where he lays next to Frank's school desk. Bocce is special, and because he is quiet in the classroom, he is allowed to stay. Sister Margaret Mary, Sister Hildagar and the others talk about it, and decide to make Bocce the school mascot. He knows his place in the classroom and he knows that the sisters are the boss. He is smart and catches on quickly. He watches as the sister erases the black-board. Every now and then she drops the eraser and picks it up. He sees this happen several times and the next time it happens, Bocce runs up to the front of the classroom, grabs the eraser and takes it to the sister.

All of the kids laugh and the sister says, "Thank you Bocce."

He wags his tail, lets out a bark, and runs back to Frank's desk.

One afternoon on his way home from school Frank and Bocce had set some traps. He had been noticing a hole near the bottom of a rotten tree trunk. Thinking he might catch a coon, he sets a trap.

The next day before school he checks them as always, and the trap by the rotten tree trunk appears to be gone. As he looks closer, what ever was in that trap has burrowed down into the hole, trap and all. He struggles to pull it out, Bocce watches closely. Then Bocce moves back and barks, which is unlike him. Frank has caught a skunk and can't get away in time. He gets sprayed. Bocce tried to tell him, but Frank didn't know. He goes on to school early as always. He sits in his regular spot by the window and Bocce in his spot. He ignores the smell that he carries with him. As the other kids come in and take their seats, the sister enters the room.

"Good morning children."

"Good morning Sister Margaret Mary."

She then says, "There must have been a skunk near-by before class started children."

The sister faces the flag and says, "Let us all remain standing and recite our Pledge of Allegiance to the Flag. Okay children, be seated and let us begin our morning prayer."

The smell is not getting any better and the kids begin holding their noses looking at one another. The sister realizes that the skunk must be hiding in the room. She begins searching and finds nothing. As she walks around the room and nears Frank, the smell gets stronger. She realizes that Frank has it all over his clothes.

Frank is questioned, "Frank were you in the woods again this morning?"

"Yes Sister, I couldn't help it. When I pulled the trap out of the hole, this big skunk sprayed me and..."

The sister interrupts, "Frank, the whole classroom smells because of you. Now I am going to have to move the children into Sister Hildagars room until the smell clears out of my classroom. You need to go home and get cleaned up."

He leaves and Bocce follows, but he stays a few feet behind.

When he reaches home, he yells for his mother from outside the house. She comes out and immediately smells the skunk. Frank is distressed from this whole situation. He tells her what happened.

She says, "Frank you know the old watering trough in the barn? Go back there and start emptying the water out of it and wait for me there."

She goes to the kitchen and starts warming buckets of water.

While she is doing that, she sees Vincenzo walking towards the house dragging a deer. She doesn't want to bother him, she continues to do what she is doing. Vincenzo hangs the deer on a tree and walks inside.

Unaware of what is going on he asks, "What are you doing?"

Antonetta explains, "Frank got sprayed by a skunk and the sister sent him home from school because he stunk up the classroom."

"Where is he?"

"I told him to go wait in the barn for me. He stunk so bad I didn't want to let him in the house," Antonetta said.

Vincenzo walks down to the cellar and picks out about ten large jars of crushed tomatoes that they had canned for winter. There appears to be well over a hundred jars so taking ten will not hurt their supply. He takes them up stairs, opens them and mixes them in the water that is warming on the stove. They begin to carry their concoction out to the barn making several trips back and forth until they have enough so that Frank is able to lay down with his body submerged in the mixture. The air is cold and the water is steaming. I watch as they pour the contents into the trough.

"You got into the wrong hole Frank, you got out-smarted. Take off your clothes and get in the tub," Vincenzo said.

Vincenzo walks outside and starts a fire and warms more water for the trough and Antonetta gets more crushed tomatoes. Frank stays in the tub and soaks for a couple of more hours. When they are done warming the water and Vincenzo figures he has been in there long enough, he throws Frank's clothes in to the fire. It's lucky that Bocce was smart enough not to get sprayed or else he would have been in that tub of hot tomatoes with Frank, and I don't think he would have liked that very much. Antonetta wraps Frank in a towel and they run inside where Frank can take a real bath. Antonetta has the tub filled with laundry soap and he soaks for another hour or so. It's almost supper time and Vincenzo is back skinning the deer that he shot. What a day it has been.

Vincenzo tells Frank, "You should have known that if Bocce wouldn't get near that hole there must have been something wrong."

Frank always loves to explore with Bocce by his side of course.

Looking for arrow heads along the Spring Garden or the Passaic River, he occasionally jumps in for a swim on a hot summer day. It doesn't matter where, he is always curious in what is beyond the next hill or where a stream or river would end. He loves secret hiding places in the barns and even the house.

In the old homestead, there is a set of stairs in a closet that leads to an attic. Vincenzo and Antonetta store things up here. The attic is finished as though someone may have lived here once. Frank loves to come up here and play. One day while playing he discovers a door behind some things stacked against a wall. It's not a regular size door. It's about a two by three foot hatch, nailed to the wall. He gently knocks, it sounds hollow. He begins prying, finally pulling it loose from the wall. He peers inside. There is a crawl space that looks as though it goes about three feet and stops at another wall. When he reaches the wall, there is another hatch. He knocks again, and it is hollow. He pries and breaks it loose. Inside there is a light shining through an attic vent. It appears to be a full size room big enough to stand up and walk around in. He enters the room and waits, as his eyes get adjusted to the dimness of the room. As he looks closer, this room is a place that existed in another time. He seems a little hesitant to go any further. He feels as though maybe he shouldn't be in here. The silence of the room is suddenly broken when a mouse scurries across the floor, scaring him enough to want to turn back. He grabs his composure and continues on. There in a corner is what appears to be a blue Civil War military uniform, hanging neatly in front of a large mirror, and furniture from the same era that is still neatly placed around the room, as though someone is still living here. There is a comb, a straight razor, and some old coins neatly arranged on a bureau. On the wall there is an old infantry man's flint lock musket with the date of 1863 etched below the hammer. Under the musket on the same wall hangs a fine looking sword with fancy etchings on it. He sits and tries to imagine who's things these could be. Without moving anything, he crawls back out and places the things that his parents have stored in their proper place.

At supper he asks his father if he knew about the room. Vincenzo said that he knew that there was a crawl space but he thought that it ended there. He said that when he bought the house, it had been empty for a couple of years and that the person who owned it was a man that lived alone and very rarely left the house. Vincenzo said that the man lived here until the day he died. Vincenzo guessed that these things must have been his.

I remembered the musket and the sword as a boy. When we were children my father had them hanging in his basement and he told us the story of how he found them upstairs in the old homestead along with some other things. Now, I knew that the story was true.

A couple of years go by. In winter Vincenzo continues to hunt for food and trap for extra money. In the spring and summer he works on the estates around Madison. He feels that he needs more help. He needs Frank's help. There is not enough time in the day to get everything done working alone. Vincenzo insists that hard work is the only way that you can get ahead in life. Being uneducated himself, he doesn't seem to think that school is that important, so he decides to pull Frank out of school. The sisters hate to see him go and even attempt to talk to Vincenzo. But it doesn't help. His mind is made up. I can tell Frank misses school and everyone misses him and Bocce. He doesn't lose touch with the kids or the sisters that taught him. The sisters tell Frank to come by and visit anytime he wants, and that Bocce can come too. From time to time when they have a chance, he and Bocce do visit.

Once or twice a year, the nurse from the foundling comes by. She never lets on who she is. Frank still continues to think that she is a friend of the family.

Now Frank is able to spend more time helping his father working on the estates, and more time hunting and trapping. No matter what time of year, they are always up at 4:30. Today they are going squirrel hunting. I follow them to Spring Garden. After a couple of hours, they figure there is enough for supper. They come home, skin, clean them, and give them to Antonetta. She will cook an excellent meal while they go off to work on the Ward's Estate.

On the top of a hillside on the estate stands a giant clock tower made of stone. It has to be over a hundred feet tall. Inside is a spiral staircase that leads to the top of the tower to an observation deck. On days that they get there early enough, before work, Frank climbs to the top of the tower, today is one of those days. I follow and watch him and Bocce. Once at the top he leans on the rail. I can tell that he is day dreaming as he scans the New York City skyline, which seems so far away, but in fact is only twenty four miles away.

From this point, looking in the other direction you can see all the beautiful rolling hills of north central New Jersey.

He stays in one spot and I wonder what he is thinking.

Then I hear Vincenzo, "Frank come on down. It's time for work."

Without a word, Frank turns around and heads down the tower.

After a hard days work at the Ward's estate, they silently walk side by side back to their horse and buggy and head home.

As we near the house, Vincenzo says, "Smell the air Frank, it's your mother's sauce."

Frank says, "I'm hungry pop."

Antonetta has been cooking the sauce since this morning.

Everything is from the garden. First she fried the squirrel legs that Vincenzo and Frank left with her this morning in olive oil, then she adds a little bit of garlic and oregano and fries them until they are a golden brown. Then she puts them in the homemade sauce where everything simmers over a slow heat all day. The smell permeates the house. At supper time everything is poured on to the macaroni and Vincenzo reaches under the table next to his chair for his jug of red wine.

After working a variety of jobs, Vincenzo undertakes the job of tearing down the old one room-red brick schoolhouse that Frank had gone to a few years earlier. Always economically-minded, Vincenzo uses the bricks to build a brick house for his wine cellar. I had remembered the brick house when I was a boy. By then it was no longer being used, and it was nearly abandoned except for a few barrels of wine that had turned to vinegar. Now I was having a chance to see it as it was used back then.

Walking up the long pathway towards the brick house, a gust of wind brings a sweet smell. I open the door, and the center of the building is completely open. Inside, the perimeter of the building is surrounded with barrels of wine and catwalks about three feet wide in front of the barrels. The staircase, inside the entryway, goes down about ten steps with more catwalks and wine barrels. As I continue, another set of stairs takes me back up and out a back door.

As I leave the brick house, I notice how cold it is. Even though it is the middle of March, I'm in the same clothes I was in when I arrived. Freezing, I decide to take a closer look at the glass greenhouse which stands next to the brick house. I run up to the entrance and let myself in. There is an aisle the length of the greenhouse. To the left and right of the aisle, are shelves also the length of the greenhouse filled with very fine soil. I can smell the richness of the soil. I continue to walk down the aisle to where a coal stove is. Not too far from the stove is a fig tree. As I warm myself near the stove, I hear a sound and quickly turn to look. I find Vincenzo and my father walking in with bags of seeds and they immediately start to plant.

Vincenzo tells my father, "Frank these seeds will get a good start here. In a couple of months, the plants will be big enough and the weather will be warm enough to transplant everything outside."

Antonetta walks in and begins to do her chores. She shovels coal in to the already warm stove and it soon feels as though it's about seventy degrees. Antonetta finishes in the greenhouse and heads toward the chicken coop to collect eggs. Next to the chicken coop is the pig-pen with two large pigs lying down in the back corner and next to that is the barn with Blacky the workhorse sharing hay with Gertrude the milk cow. The dirt in the garden is tilled and appears to be ready for planting. In a few months, a large variety of vegetables from tomatoes to eggplants, head and leaf lettuce, escarole, rows and rows of stringbeans, onions, garlic, and herbs of all kinds, will be ready to be picked.

Frank walks out of the greenhouse and starts looking in the trees. I can't figure out what he is doing.

Then he begins to call out names as he scans the tree line, "Pat, Mike!" he calls.

I wonder what he is doing. Then all of a sudden two gray squirrels make their way through the trees jumping from limb to limb and climb to Frank's shoulder. He reaches into his pocket and gives them each a walnut. Being in the woods a lot Frank finds injured animals from time to time. He has a soft heart and takes them home until they are well enough to be set free. Evidently, these squirrels liked the treatment they received and decided to stay close by. These two squirrels were off limits to the frying pan and Antonetta's sauce.

When the squirrels scamper away, a big black crow with one leg that Frank helped when it was a baby, soars down crowing and making a racket, also looking for a handout. They all reside in the trees that surround the old homestead.

The next day, I see the Twombly Estate which my father used to talk about. It is everything I expected. There are three Silver Ghost Rolls-Royce's parked in the circular driveway in front of the mansion.

They seem to have parties all the time. It's amazing to see all of the things my father told us stories about. Even more important, I continue to see my father and his father relate to one another. I never met my grandfather because he died when I was a year old. I had only seen photos, so to hear his voice and see his facial expressions was remarkable. I love his strong Italian accent and when he speaks to my father, half of what he says is in Italian. By now my father speaks and understands Italian very well. So Frank knows both languages.

As time passes, I find myself doing everything my father and grandfather do. No one ever notices me except that one time at the foundling when my father smiled at me. I'm starting to wonder if I even exist. It's frustrating to be here and not be able to be heard or seen.

In October of 1920, Frank turns fifteen. The leaves are beginning to change as fall is here. The days are sunny, bright and beautiful and the air is crisp and cool. There always seems to be a gentle wind at this time of year.

About a week or so after my father's birthday, everyone gets up at the usual time. I notice something different right away. Something is missing. Every morning, Bocce would run excitedly around the house and into Frank's room and jump on the bed and start licking his face.

My father notices that something is wrong.

Frank yells, "Bocce, here boy!"

Frank listens intently for the sounds of Bocce's paws against the hardwood floors, but there is nothing. He gets up from his bed and looks down. On the floor, next to his bed, is Bocce laying on his side. Bocce sadly looks straight up at Frank and tries to wag his tail.

He can barely keep his head up.

I know what is happening, I really don't want to see this, but where can I go?

Frank tells his friend, "Come on boy lets go eat breakfast!"

Bocce still doesn't get up.

"Please Bocce, please get up!"

Antonetta hears Frank talking and comes into the room. She sees Bocce and calls Vincenzo. Vincenzo gently picks Bocce up and lays him on the bed. They all sit with him. With everything in his being, Frank hugs Bocce. He tries to comfort his little friend.

Vincenzo and Antonetta sit in silence, as they know what is happening.

"Oh Bocce, please don't go, I love you so much, your my best friend!" Frank cries.

Frank leans over and lays his head on Bocce's little body.

He wants to be as close to him as can get. Bocce looks at him with loving eyes and returns the hug by licking him on the face, as if to say, "Thank you for being my friend, and for such a wonderful life."

Frank sits back up and Vincenzo places Bocce on Frank's lap.

Tears are rolling down Antonetta's face as she quietly cries. I cry as I watch Vincenzo, this big proud man struggling to hold back his tears.

A few minutes later Bocce lets his head fall down on to Frank's lap, closes his eyes, and silently dies.

Antonetta lunges forward to hug and comfort Frank.

Vincenzo says, "Bocce is in heaven now Frank, and we will all see him again someday."

Frank lost his best friend today. A friend he will never forget.

A friend that had been with him since he was three years old. He was a friend that stuck by him no matter what. Through all kinds of weather, no matter how cold, how deep the snow, or how hard the rain, Bocce was there. Bocce was with him when he got sprayed by that skunk, which seemed so long ago. Frank's sadness leaves him for a moment, as he remembers when the sisters at school would scold Bocce for disrupting the class. He would run away, only to come right back because he just wanted to be near Frank. He was a friend that protected him. He would miss him riding in his basket on the front of his bicycle so proud, as all the old timers and store owners in town waved when they rode by.

The three of them take Bocce outside and wrap him in one of his old favorite blankets and bury him under the apple tree next to the brick house with his name and the date he died chiseled into a flat rock.

Bocce My Beloved Friend Died 1920

This spot was the family's favorite place to sit when the weather was nice and it was Bocce's favorite spot too. They plant daffodils over the grave. Those daffodils still come up every year to this day.

They say a prayer and Frank tries to imagine what Bocce is doing in heaven. He hoped that he wouldn't be lonesome up there. Then they walk hand in hand back to the house.

Frank doesn't ride his bicycle for a long time. He parks it under the apple tree next to Bocce's grave. Things seemed so different without his little friend next to him. He visits the school one day and sees Sister Hildagar. She is always happy to see him.

"Hello Frank," she said. "It's so nice to see you, I haven't seen you in quite some time. How have you been?"

"I'm fine, I guess."

The sister senses that something is wrong and asks, "Frank are you sure?"

"Yes Sister, I have been very busy lately working with my father."

"Do you like working with your father?"

"I love being with my parents." Frank replies.

"Where is everyone's favorite little friend Bocce?" Sister Hildager asks.

A tear rolls down his cheek as he calmly tells her what happened.

The sister hugs him as a tear rolls down her cheek and says, "Oh Frank, I know you lost your best friend, but think about all of the happy times you and everyone had with him. When we lose a loved one in life no matter who, a parent, a sister, a brother or a little dog, life must go on, no matter what, and we need to cherish all those wonderful memories and never let them go. Frank you are a special boy, with a good heart. Don't you ever change. I know that Bocce was very special."

"Do you think he's in heaven Sister?"

She looks at him and says, "Frank, heaven is what you make it. If you believe he is there, then he is, and yes Frank, I believe he is with God now and he will be okay."

#

I'm not sure what is happening, but my surroundings begin to look hazy and blurred. I can hardly see Frank. I'm being pushed forward and everything in front of me begins to speed up. Within a flash I'm back in my house in my father's favorite chair. I feel drained and still have tears in my eyes. I look at the clock and realize that no time has passed at all for me. I had been with my father for years. It is a strange realization. Fatigued, I fall asleep in the chair. When I wake up the next morning, I wonder why I came back. I loved those times. I don't want to live in the present anymore. What did I do wrong? Why wasn't I able to stay and continue what I started? My journey to the past.

Chapter Five

The Seventh Round

Noticing that I had the same clothes on, I decided to change. The clothes had been new when I was back there, but now they are old and shabby.

I continue to look at piles of census. I want so much to be back there. Times were so much different back then. Things seemed to be more peaceful and I missed everyone. I keep thinking why did I come back?

This didn't make any sense to come back now. I had to do something to get back there. I wasn't going to let this go, I was determined. As I look at all the records I have, I finally realize that when I left, it was 1920. The latest census I have is 1920. I know that there must be a correlation. I have to get more census beyond 1920. I figure that any any records will work, city directories, old phone books, anything. I go to the library and look for the 1925 state census or the 1930 federal census. My search seems hopeless. I can't find either.

Confused, I ask the librarian, "Can you tell me where I might find the census of New Jersey after the year 1920?"

To my horror, she says, "Those census have not been released yet."

In frustration I ask, "What records do you have after the year 1920?"

"Well we do have some old phone books and quite a few city directories from that time."

I grab every record that I can find and make copies. I bring them home and put the clothes I had on before. I want to reenact what I had done before. I close all the blinds and windows in the house to shut out any outside noises. The room is dark, I sit in my father's chair with one hand on the records and the other hand gripping my old lucky penny. I close my eyes and wait. Nothing happens. Frustrated, I close my eyes again and concentrate on everything that I had seen when I was there before. I imagine everyone's faces. I imagine all the places, the school, the town, and how it looked then. Then I imagine the old homestead and how it looked when I left there.

#

Suddenly the present starts to fade in and out and seconds later I am flung back to what seems to be early spring. It is a clear and mild day, and I am on the front porch of the old homestead sitting in a rocking chair. Things don't seem to look much different. The cornfield is still across the street but the corn hasn't been planted yet. I get up and look around. Clearly this is a different time. The fruit trees have grown in size from what I remembered. As I walk around to the back, I hear men's voices. As I look near the barn in the back, I notice what appears to be a boxing ring with a few people watching as two young fellows are in the ring, battling it out with one another. I walk closer and as I do, one of the fellows falls to the ground.

Looking closer, I see that the fellow standing up is my father. The referee looks like he might be a friend. In fact they all look like friends about the same ages.

Then a familiar smell hits me. The smell that I love is coming from inside the house. I walk into the kitchen. When the door opens, everyone sees it open, but they don't see me and they don't seem to care. They look for a moment, but just go on with their business.

Antonetta is cooking and Vincenzo is sitting in his chair at the kitchen table with his red wine. As always, the jug is on the floor next to him. They haven't changed much in looks, maybe just a little older. As I look at the calendar on the kitchen wall, it is March 1927. I can hear the sound of beautiful music coming from the other room. I follow the sound to the living room and there on the table is a wind up old fashion victrola. As I look and listen closer, I realize that Enrico Caruso is singing all of the old Neapolitan Italian love songs that I remembered so well growing up.

I make my way back to the kitchen. Vincenzo and Antonetta are still there and Frank comes in. He is no longer a boy, he is 22 years old now. He has turned out to be a fine young man. They sit and Antonetta serves them supper. Then she sits, and Frank talks about how much he likes boxing and how great Jack Dempsey was before he lost to Gene Tunney in 1926. From the conversation, I gather that Frank is pretty good at the sport. When I was growing up, I recall some of the old timers discussing the days when they were young and how they would go to Frank's house. They would go on to talk about the boxing ring in the Sapio's back-yard.

"Saturday afternoon fights, All Challengers Welcome." Read the sign on the barn next to the ring.

There are burlap bags full of sand secured tightly with manila rope hanging from a tree near the barn. Closer to the ring there is a covered structure where Frank is practicing on a speed bag. Although primitive looking, this informal training camp serves its purpose.

The word gets around quickly if there is going to be a good fight. Everyone knows who the good fighters are. There are some pretty tough characters around town. Frank has been the local champ for a little over a year now. Everyone knows him and I think he would have made something out of his talent, if it wasn't for the fellow from the next town over. His name is Tommy Bavitt. He is a few years older than Frank and he is tough! His knuckles are all smashed and callused. His nose has been broken a couple of times and he has a bad case of cauliflower ears.

Again, I find myself at the ring. There is quite a crowd for this one. It is to be a ten round fight. Both fighters arrive and ignore one another. They take their corners. Frank spars anxiously with the air in front of him. He's as fast as a bullet, and he is known for his lighting speed and come-out of nowhere left uppercut. As long as he can stay away, this guy shouldn't be a problem for him. Bavitt has his back turned and he is pulling on the ropes. It seems as though the whole ring shakes when he does this. Even my father notices his strength. The referee, also a fighter gets in the middle of the ring and introduces both fighters as being undefeated. Bavitt has never once turned around since his arrival and continues pulling on the ropes. Frank is pacing as if to say, "Lets get on with it." The referee calls them to the center of the ring. Tommy Bavitt finally turns and they both walk to the center. They look intensely at one another, eye to eye, nose to nose, each with a cold stare as the referee gives them their instructions. Bavitt looks like a bulldog with his face all battered from his previous fights. Although they appear to be the same height and nearly the same weight, he seems bigger boned and just a little bit heavier looking then Frank. But this will be a good match because of Frank's speed.

The referee tells them to shake hands, return to their corners, and at the bell, come out fighting. The bell rings and the fight begins.

Round one is uneventful. They are both good. It seems as though Frank is studying his opponent. Frank seems as though he is the smarter boxer in his moves and thinking. While not taking anything away from Tommy, he seems to be more of a bruiser with more strength.

Round two begins and both fighters seem as though they have figured one another out, as they both come out swinging and equally landing several punches. As the fight continues it intensifies.

In the third round, Frank lands his famous come-out of nowhere left upper cut to Bavitt's jaw, followed by a right, and another left.

Bavitt falls against the ropes and wobbles to the ground. By the count of three he is up. He shakes his head to get his senses back and snorts through his nose with a rough harsh sound. The bell rings for the fighters to retreat to their respective corners.

It's the sixth round and it's a good one, as both fighters trade punches relentlessly. If I were a judge, I would call this match a draw so far. The locals are going wild as they knew that this would be what they expected. Frank with his speed and cunning moves, and Tommy with his power, set the stage for a good match. The bell rings and both fighters are tired and worn. They sit in their corners.

With four rounds to go, the bell rings for the seventh round. The fighters come out looking at one another in the eyes. So far Frank has been able to stay away from Tommy's powerful punches. It's about two minutes in to the round and the fierce battle continues, when all of a sudden, Bavitt comes around with a right hook and hits Frank in the right ear! I and the others could actually hear the impact when it hit Frank. It doesn't look good. This was what he needed to stay away from. He falls to the ground and lays there to the count of six. Trying to get up, he is so dazed with blood coming out of his right ear, he lays right back down. Everything around him is blurred and he hears a constant ringing noise in his head from that brutal punch. The voices from all the onlookers seem so distant and muffled. This is the end of Frank's fighting career. His eardrum is broken from the punch.

From then on he was deaf in that ear. Antonetta didn't like boxing and was always worried that Frank would get hurt. Vincenzo on the other hand didn't care one way or the other, though he did think that it was good experience to know how to fight.

I remember seeing Tommy Bavitt when he was much older. He would walk down Main Street in Madison shadow boxing at his reflection in the store windows. Then he would make his way into Charlie's luncheonette on Waverly Place and sit in the back corner booth by himself. He rarely spoke to anyone. Charlie would give him a cup of coffee, then he would get up and leave. He seemed as though he may have been pretty punchy.

There was a sadness about him. He looked worn out.

One day I spoke to him and said, "My name is Tom Sapio. My father is Frank Sapio. Do you remember him? He was a fighter like you."

He didn't answer for about a minute. He kept looking at me with a cold stare. His eyes were cloudy and appeared to be swollen. He thought for a while and in a slurred rough voice he said, "Do you want to fight me? I remember him as a good fighter. I fought him. Are you a fighter?

I'll fight you! When do you want to fight? I'll fight you right now," he said.

He stood up as though he was going to take a swing at me!

I quickly said, "No I'm not a fighter, I just wanted to meet you I heard that you were a good fighter."

He said, "I still am! I'll fight anybody!"

I'm sure he would, I thought to myself.

I was about fifteen at the time. He had to be in his late sixties and he still wanted to fight. Then he took his last swig of coffee got up and walked out. As he was walking he sort of staggered and was taking short jabs at the air in front of him and swerving as though he was dodging punches.

Now that Frank was forced to give up boxing, he spends more time again with his father trapping, hunting and working on the estates.

After work one day Vincenzo and Frank come home. Vincenzo sits down in his usual spot under the apple tree where Bocce is buried. I notice that Bocce's grave is still there and very well kept with flowers.

Antonetta is inside cooking supper. Frank checks the family's mail as always, because

Vincenzo and Antonetta still had not learned how to read or write. Frank notices that one of the letters is from Italy.

They always got letters from relatives in Italy. Antonetta comes outside and they gather around the apple tree. Frank opens it and begins to read out loud.

> "Dear Vincenzo,
>
> I am writing this letter to inform you that our father Antonio has been sick since he collapsed several weeks ago. The physician, has told us that his heart is weak and that he has developed pneumonia and will most likely die soon. Since I returned to Marigliano many years ago, mama has been saddened and talks of you often. She misses you Vincenzo. She says that she would love to see you once before she dies."
>
> Vincenzo's face turns to sorrow and pain when he hears this about his mother.
>
> Then Frank reads on, "Even with age and sickness brought on by his collapse, our father has not changed in his ways of thinking. He is bed ridden and mama does what she can to help him, for she has always been a good wife and mother. If your finances allow you to return home this would make our mother very happy.
>
> Your brother, Feligia."

Vincenzo decides that maybe he should make the trip. He hates leaving Antonetta,

Frank, the homestead and all of his accomplishments.

But he thinks of the last time he saw his mother, when he sat next to her in church that day, and this saddens him. If it were not for those thoughts and those words in the letter that Feligia wrote about his mother, he would stay and go on with his life.

He has taught Frank well. He knows that Frank will take care of everything while he is gone. He applies for an emergency passport and leaves for Italy the next week. I follow Vincenzo. The Port of New York is still busy with new immigrants arriving into the country. Vincenzo never thought that he would return to Italy and I can tell that he really does not want to make this trip.

After a lengthy voyage across the Atlantic, we arrive at the same dock in Italy that Vincenzo had left from so many years ago. It hasn't changed, there is still a heavy influx of people leaving Italy looking for a better life in America.

Vincenzo rents a horse and buggy. He remembers his way to the village. It will take about an hour to get there. It's the same old dusty road, that takes him through the peaceful hills and villages where he grew up. Nothing has changed. The hillsides are still covered with olive orchards and grape vineyards. As he gets closer, he can see his old house in the distance, and it hasn't changed either. Then he notices an old woman hanging clothes with her back turned to him. He knows that this is his mother Rosa. She has aged. She seems a little frail from what I remembered in the early days. She does not see him at first. She turns to look as she hears the buggy wheels on the dirt road. As the buggy approaches the house Vincenzo raises his hand and waves. He gets out of the buggy and his mother now realizes it's her son Vincenzo. She drops what she is doing. Vincenzo walks to his mother. She can't believe her eyes.

"Mama," he says.

Evidently, Feligia never told their mother that he had written Vincenzo a letter, because if Vincenzo did not come, then Rosa would not be disappointed. So she is completely surprised!

They hug and Rosa says, "Vincenzo, I am so glad you came, not a day goes by that I don't think of you. I've missed you so much Vincenzo, I pray for you everyday. You were my first son and you were always a good boy. I am so sorry that things could not have been different. I have always loved you Vincenzo. I feel like it is partly my fault that you left..."

Vincenzo interrupts and gently says, "It wasn't you mama."

Vincenzo's emotions are conflicting. He had such a bad childhood here, yet he loved his mother very much. Compounding this, he never heard his mother say she loved him. Vincenzo was happy to hear these words, but he knew that his life was in America now with his family. As they walk to the backyard, he sees one of his brothers and some other relatives sitting at a table under some grapevines talking. Everyone is glad to see him. They talk for a while and Feligia shows up. As always he is well dressed. He is glad that Vincenzo has come back home, if for no other reason than to make their mother happy.

Rosa says, "Feligia how come you didn't tell me you wrote to Vincenzo?"

"I wanted you to be surprised, and I didn't know if Vincenzo would come mama."

They continue to talk and catch up. Vincenzo asks Feligia,

"What have you been doing with yourself, you still dress real nice."

"I'm in the olive oil business," he answers.

Vincenzo notices that Feligia is wearing a small pistol under his jacket. He asks, "What are you doing with that, do you use that to guard the olive trees?"

They laugh, and Feligia answers, "Vincenzo, you know how it is, you have to protect yourself."

Just then, a voice, Antonio's voice, from inside the house calls out, "Who's out there?"

Vincenzo's brother says, "It's nothing pop."

They continue talking, everyone wants to know about America.

Feligia asks how Antonetta and Frank are. Vincenzo says that they are fine, and that Frank has turned out to be a good son.

He says, "We do everything together. He is taking care of everything while I'm here. I bought a couple of pieces of property with a house on both of the properties and we have a little farm. We live about a mile from town. It's a good town, there's a lot of work there."

Rosa sits quietly listening to Vincenzo.

Vincenzo looks at her, and how she has aged.

"Mama are you okay?"

She looks at him and says, "I was just thinking, I'm so glad you married a nice Italian girl Vincenzo, I remember Antonetta when they lived here, she was always a hard worker."

"I know mama, she helps me with everything," Vincenzo replied.

Again, Antonio's voice from inside the house calls out, "Who's out there? I want to know who in the hell is out there! God damm it!"

Feligia says, "Wait a minute pop, I'm coming!"

Vincenzo goes in with Feligia. He sees his father on his deathbed. Old and sick with pneumonia and a little bit blind, his father hasn't changed much. He is still mean, and he looks mean. He strains his eyes as he is trying to make out who it is.

"Who's there? I don't see so good," Antonio said.

Feligia replies, "It's Vincenzo pop."

Antonio asks, "Who? You have to come closer so I can see."

Vincenzo says, "It's your son."

"My son, which one?"

Vincenzo replies, "It's Vincenzo, your son from America!"

Without so much as a hello, Antonio begins yelling at Vincenzo for leaving them so many years ago.

He says, "You no good son of a bitch! What are you doing here?

Did you come here to go to work? There's no work for you here you bum!

I heard you have a family, I don't give a damm about them either!"

Vincenzo kind of expected that this would be the type of reception he would receive from his father. Feligia was right. He had not changed. He was as mean as ever. Vincenzo doesn't say anything else, he just listens as his father carries on. He finally walks out of the room. Everyone outside could hear Antonio, so they knew what was going on.

Feligia tells Vincenzo, "Don't worry about him Vincenzo, he's like that with everybody and besides you came here to see ma."

"I will never figure him out and why he was so mean. I never did anything to him," Vincenzo said.

Rosa never interfered years ago, and she doesn't interfere now.

She knows that she has no say so, especially, when Antonio speaks.

Vincenzo never goes back to his father's room, he spends most of his time with his mother. Vincenzo stays for a few more days, but There is nothing for him here. His home is in America. He misses Antonetta, Frank, the homestead, and his farm. I think he wishes that his mother could come back to America with him, but she is old, set in her ways and she would never leave her husband. His stay in Italy is shorter than the time it took to get here. He will miss his mother Rosa. He tells her that he needs to get back to his family.

She understands his responsibility. Vincenzo listens as she tells him, "Oh Vincenzo I didn't think that I would ever see you again. You have always been dear to my heart. I know you love your family, you take care of them and treat your son good, that is important. I will pray for you like I have always prayed for you Vincenzo."

The next morning Vincenzo tells his mother good-bye. Being a man of few words, his eyes tell the story of how he feels.

He only tells her, "Mama please take care of yourself. I will miss you." He knows that he will never see his mother again.

Vincenzo is so glad to be back in Madison, Antonetta and Frank wonder how his trip was, He doesn't say much, just that nothing had changed.

Three months pass before Vincenzo receives another letter from Italy. The letter explains that his father died five days after he left and his mother had passed away a month later from a broken heart.

Vincenzo mourns when he hears this, but he is glad that he got to see his mother.

As time goes by, Vincenzo keeps telling Frank that he needs to learn a trade.

"Frank, I don't want you to do what I do, for the rest of your life. I work from day to day never knowing when they might say we don't need you anymore. Someday things will change around here Frank, they will build houses here, and you won't be able to hunt for food like we do now."

Frank decides to make his living as a painter and interior decorator. He works in all the beautiful homes and estates in and around Madison. All of the wealthy people learn of Frank's good taste, patience and know how in selecting colors and wall paper to go with their decor.

He begins to do very well and has more than enough work to keep him busy and he very rarely refuses a job. Although there is a waiting list, people are willing to wait for him. On weekends, Frank still finds time to trap. Fur coats are still very popular and not too many people know the technique of trapping. This is good extra money for Frank.

Chapter Six

When A Candle Burns Down

Most all of the Italians in Madison had come from the same part of Italy, in and around the little towns and villages surrounding Naples. Everyone in Madison seems to know one another from the other side, or they may have known their families over there. I guess the word continued to get around, that Madison is a good place to live at this time because new families continue to make Madison their home.

There is one man by the name of Giuseppe DiPalma from the village of Somma Vesuviana, which is not too far from Marigliano and close to the great Mount Vesuvius. He has been friends with Vincenzo for quite a few years. Giuseppe is a quiet and good-looking man. His hair is prematurely turning white, but this just adds to his sophisticated appearance. It also contrasts well with his olive skin. The families, also knew one another on the other side. Giuseppe has a wife and children still in Italy and he misses them. Giuseppe's wife is about third or fourth cousins to Vincenzo. Giuseppe has been coming back and forth from Italy for some time now. He works for a while, makes some money and returns to Europe. While in Madison, he lives for a time as a boarder in the Italian section of town at the bottom of North Street.

I'm walking down North Street, when all of a sudden everything starts to blur and I'm being pulled backwards.

#

Suddenly I appear to be in a different time again. I'm still in Madison, but I am no longer with Vincenzo, Antonetta or Frank. I am standing outside of one of the many greenhouses in Madison.

One of the greenhouses in Madison is called Totty's. I had always heard, from my mother that the roses grown at Toddy's were sent all around the world. This is an upscale place. The rows of glass greenhouses which are lined up next to one another, seem to be at least fifty yards long. I walk in and the odor is like perfume. There are thousands of carnations and chrysanthemums from one end of the greenhouse to the other. I see The calendar on the wall from Burnet's Hardware Store, it's 1924. I enter another greenhouse, and this one is full of rosebushes. There, pruning the roses is Giuseppe. He is a professional rose grower. On one of his recent trips to Italy, he had given his wife money to put with the rest of the money they had been saving through the years, so that she and the children could come join him in America someday.

#

As I open the door and walk out of the greenhouse, the surroundings no longer look like Madison. Before closing the door behind me, I turn to look once more and I can still see Giuseppe pruning roses. I close the door and begin walking. I walk about twenty feet or so and turn again to look behind me. The greenhouse is no longer there. I realize by the change of the landscape that I am in Italy. There, in the not to far distance is the smoldering, Mount Vesuvius. As I continue to walk, I'm drawn to an attractive, well kept, small, two-story, stone house surrounded with fruit trees and vegetable gardens. There in the yard is an old woman. She is wearing black, with a black shawl, a black kerchief and her face is weathered. Although she is tall, She walks with a stoop. I imagine she got like this from years and years of bending over picking vegetables. She must be Rachele, Concetta's mother and my great-grandmother. I walk inside and there in the kitchen I see Concetta. She is tall, and a very pretty personable woman with a medium complexion and a beautiful speaking voice. The DiPalma's have six children. Mike is the oldest, followed by Anne, Tommy, Mary, Jimmy, and Nancy. The children are all very young.

I remembered the calendar back at the greenhouse. If this is still 1924, then Anne, my mother would be ten years old. She is a charming little girl with hazel eyes and light brown hair that is pulled up. She is wearing a plaid peasant like dress. She walks to a window that faces a path that leads to the little village of Somma Vesuviana. She leans on the stone windowsill and peers down the path as though she is day dreaming. I walk over and stand behind her. I can see the village there in the distance. There is a group of people walking towards the house. Rachele comes into the house with a load of vegetables.

Anne looks away from the window and says, "Mama everyone is coming!"

Concetta says, "Okay Anne set the table."

All of the children are helping in one way or another. I don't know any of these people that are walking down the path. They must be cousins, aunts and uncles. It appears that some of the children are the same age, and they are all very well mannered. I can't help but notice that all the women are wearing black. I had always heard that Italian women dress in black for many years after a loved one dies.

One of the aunts tells Concetta's children, "You're so lucky you are going to America tomorrow. Don't forget your cousins in Italy, and please write us when you can."

Everyone sits for dinner and they say a prayer. They pray that their journey to America is a safe one, and that their new life will be prosperous.

From what I can gather, this is going to be the last time that this family will be together.

Concetta will miss her mother, she tells her, "Mama, when we get settled, we will send for you."

Rachele doesn't say anything, she just smiles.

Concetta knows deep in her heart her mother will never leave Italy. Rachele is old and she is use to her life in Somma. Rachele's husband had died a few years earlier and she wants to be buried next to him. Concetta and her mother seem to be very close. Concetta will miss her the most. Everyone is sad, but they know that Giuseppe is a good provider and that Concetta and her children will be okay. Tomorrow they will board the ship headed for New York. Concetta's brother and a sister along with Rachele will take them to the docks to see them off.

Upon reaching the docks, Concetta holds her youngest child Nancy in her arms. She gives strict instructions to the other children to hold hands and to stay close to her. Once on board ship, they look back at the docks and see Rachele standing there watching. Concetta holds Nancy's hand up and tells the other children to wave to their grandmother. Rachele spots them and waves back. Concetta knows that they will never see one another again. Rachele and Concetta's eyes well up with tears. Anne notices this and she gets closer to her mother and hugs her. She also begins to cry. Mike stands in silence. The other children are too young to understand. They don't realize that they will never see their family in Italy again.

The ship pulls away from the docks and Concetta looks at her mother until she can no longer see her. She already feels as though Somma is now a lifetime away.

The trip is long and there are many storms along the way. The children remain by their mother's side all the way, Concetta is very protective. Where one goes they all go.

In the morning hours of June 10th, 1924, the weather clears as they enter New York Harbor. It's a beautiful summer morning as the ship sounds its horn and they sail past the Statue of Liberty. Concetta and her kids have never seen anything like this, they are in awe. When they reach Ellis Island, the hustle and bustle there confuses the children.

Concetta isn't sure where to go. Again, as she did when they boarded the ship in Italy, she tells the children to hold hands and not let go for any reason. She tells them to wait for her while she goes to find out what they are supposed to do next. This place is packed with people and one could get lost very easily. I watch the children as they wait in silence. They look scared as they huddle together near a wall waiting for their mother to return. Concetta returns and they are glad to see her. They get through customs with no problems.

They gather their belongings and walk a distance of which seems to be about a hundred yards or so to a large dirt parking lot, filled with newly arrived immigrants waiting for familiar faces to great them.

As they are walking, there in the distance, Concetta recognizes Giuseppe standing next to an automobile. Then he too sees Concetta and his six children. He hurriedly walks to greet them and takes Concetta's bags. They all hug. It's been a long time waiting and everyone is happy that they are finally together. The automobile is a taxi that Giuseppe ordered to take them to Madison.

All of the children are very quiet, as they observe the country side and all the quaint little towns they pass. They seem to be taking everything in.

Italy was beautiful with its rolling hills, but America is beautiful in a different way. They have never seen wealth like this.

The homes are big and everything is manicured and so well kept.

Giuseppe tells everyone that they are not too far from Madison, the town that he has grown to love, and where he wants his family to be raised. He tells them that they will be living in a two story home located on Central Avenue close to a school and the center of Madison.

He tells the family that he is in the process of building a permanent home on Walnut Street, within walking distance from school.

Concetta doesn't waste any time enrolling the children in school.

She wants the best for her children. Giuseppe works long hours at the greenhouses, but he also somehow manages to work on his new house. He is there everyday and builds most of it himself. Eventually the house is completed and is ready for the family to move in. Giuseppe is so proud of his work, a pretty stucco home with a large vegetable garden and fruit trees surrounding the house. In one section of the yard is a beautiful multi-colored rose garden. The red, white and yellow roses are divided by decorative white-gravel walkways. The left and right side of the driveway is lined with red and white roses. The few neighbors that live in the area love to walk by and admire the beautiful colorful gardens that Giuseppe has created. The variety of bright colors in this yard are sight to behold. Working at Totty's as a professional rose grower for all those years gave him the experience to create his own gardens of beauty.

In the evenings after supper, the family retreats to the parlor and they listen as Concetta sings and plays Neapolitan Italian love songs on her harmonica. I had heard, when I was growing up that her voice was beautiful. Now I am really a believer. Her voice is just as I imagined it would be. She loves to talk about growing up near Mount Vesuvius. She talks of seeing the smoke coming out of the mountain every once in a while and even saw it erupt once. The children love and respect their mother and father.

Time passes quickly, it is now 1929, and Italy has become a distant memory for the children. They are all doing well in school.

Concetta walks them to school in the mornings, then she visits the church and sits by herself and prays the rosary. On Sunday mornings, they all walk to church together. Occasionally on Sunday afternoons, they visit their hometown friends Vincenzo, Antonetta and Frank.

Concetta always brings something and the families eat together and if the weather is nice, they sit on the picnic table under the apple trees. The food is so good as Concetta and Antonetta are equal in their cooking abilities. On this particular Sunday, Frank all dressed up, drives up in a brand new car. Evidently he is doing well with painting and interior decorating, plus trapping and selling furs. The children all love Frank and that flashy car that he drives. He had become friends with Mike through the years and every now and then they would ride around town together.

Before they sit down to eat, Vincenzo makes a point of telling everyone, "When you eat in this house, you will never get anything better anywhere else. Nobody can cook better than Antonetta or Concetta."

One day Concetta receives a letter from Italy telling her that her mother Rachele has passed away. She was not sick. She was picking vegetables on a Tuesday morning and dropped dead in the yard. They thought it may have been a heart attack. The family is saddened by this news. To mourn for her mother, Concetta wears black on Tuesdays and never misses mass on that day.

Back at the Sapio homestead Frank is dating a couple of girls in town, but Vincenzo doesn't approve of them. Because his father has a lot of influence on him, he stops seeing them.

Vincenzo tells Frank, "Find a nice Italian girl Frank. Italian girls will stay with you no matter what."

It's a Sunday afternoon and Frank decides that it's time for Vincenzo to learn how to drive a car.

"Pop come on outside," he says. "I want you to learn how to drive a car, times are changing you can't keep riding in that horse and buggy forever."

Vincenzo is stubborn, he tells Frank, "I don't give a damm about changing times, I'm happy with my buggy."

Frank tells him that if he learns how to drive, he can get from place to place faster.

Vincenzo thinks for a moment and finally says, "Okay I'll try it, but if I don't like it, I'm not going to do it."

Frank takes him out to the street in front of the house and shows him the basics. He tells him, "Now pop you have to start off in first gear, then when you get going faster you push the clutch in with your foot and shift it to second then third. But you have to watch where you're going, that's what this wheel is for. It will let you go this way or that way," as he points to the left and right. Frank then points to the brake and tells him, "Pop, this is important, when you want to stop you have to mash on this pedal, it's the brake. If you don't use the brake you can cause a lot of damage. Now I'm going to let you try."

Vincenzo gets in the drivers seat and Frank sits next to him in the passenger seat and I ride in the back. Vincenzo pops the clutch and floors the accelerator. He immediately loses control and drives off the road. Lucky there weren't many cars around back then, I'm sure he would have hit one.

Frank tells him, "Pop you have to slow down and do one thing at a time. You can't learn this in one day." Frustrated Vincenzo tells Frank, "I like my buggy, I just get in and the horse takes me there. I can even fall asleep if I want."

Frank insists that cars are going to take the horse and buggy's place. He says, "We can try it again tomorrow."

Frank and Vincenzo continue to practice. Vincenzo really never does catch on. He has a heavy foot and sometimes forgets to use his brake. Every now and then Frank has to grab the wheel to avoid hitting something. Even the chickens in the street know when Vincenzo is coming as they scatter when they hear the car coming up the road. As they pull into the driveway and sit for a while, Frank seems exhausted from the ride.

Frank tells Vincenzo, "Pop I don't think that this is going to work out, I'm afraid you're going to hit something. What do you think, do you want to call it quits?"

Vincenzo doesn't care one way or another, he says, "Yeah sure, what do I need to learn how to drive for! I never liked cars anyway, I like my horse and buggy."

They both agree that driving a car is not going to work, and Vincenzo goes back to his horse and buggy.

The year is 1931, and Frank has been visiting the DiPalma's quite often. He helps Giuseppe in the garden. The family thinks the world of Frank. I notice that he has turned a lot of his attention towards Anne.

She is about to turn seventeen. She has turned out to be a beautiful young lady, with light hair and fair complexion. She is a quiet girl.

When she speaks, there is a softness in her voice. I think she resembles her mother in looks and has her father's quiet personality.

Frank drives over to visit the DiPalma's. On this particular day, he pulls up into the driveway and waves hello to Giuseppe who is raking the gravel walkways in the rose garden. Not a stone is out of place. A few of the kids are helping their father while Concetta and Anne are hanging clothes out to dry. The kids notice Frank and run up to greet him. He is treated just like a brother. Being an only child and growing up with no brothers and sisters, he enjoys the attention.

After the kids are done fussing over Frank's car, Anne walks over to talk to him for a while. Frank begins the conversation by telling her how he has been trying to teach Vincenzo how to drive.

Frank says, "Pop already ran over and killed a couple of chickens. He drives too fast and he doesn't understand about the brakes. I felt bad but I had to tell him that it wasn't going to work out."

"What did he say when you told him that?" Anne asked.

"He didn't care, he said he never liked cars anyway."

Anne laughs.

Frank begins to spend a lot of time with Anne. They enjoy each others company. He asks Anne if she would like to go out on a date with him sometime.

She tells him, "Yes I would like to go, but you should probably talk to my mother and father first. If they say it's okay, then I will be happy to go."

Frank had always been comfortable around Concetta and Giuseppe, but this time he seems a little nervous. He catches Giuseppe outside one evening sitting on the front porch and nervously begins to ask him.

Giuseppe calls Concetta, and the kids listen from inside the house.

Giuseppe and Concetta love Frank, and they happily give their approval.

They call Anne outside and tell her the good news while Frank is still there on the porch with Giuseppe and Concetta. They sit and wait until Frank gets enough nerve to ask Anne out. When he finally does, there is a sigh of relief from Giuseppe and Concetta. They get up as though nothing has happened and go about their business.

The next day, Frank drives up to the house to pick Anne up. As he gets out of the car, Mike, Tommy, Mary, Jimmy and Nancy hurry out to greet him. Concetta is an old-fashioned Italian mother, who believes the whole family should go on the first few dates. They continue to see one another and as time goes by, Giuseppe and Concetta are comfortable enough to allow Frank to take Anne out alone.

In late February of 1932, Concetta begins feeling sick to her stomach. She is not one to complain or go to the doctors over every little ache and pain. She doesn't say too much to anyone about it. She thinks that maybe it's a virus of some kind. But when her illness continues, she tells Giuseppe that she thinks there is something wrong with her and that maybe she should go see the family physician, who is Dr. Eckhart. After numerous tests, Dr. Eckhart tells Giuseppe and Concetta that Concetta has developed stomach cancer and there is no cure.

He explains, "As time goes on, you will get worse. Concetta, it is hard for me to tell you this, but the kind of cancer that you have usually spreads fast. You may live from six months to a year."

The couple are devastated. Giuseppe was not one to show his emotion, but he is overwhelmed with sadness. Concetta is sad because her children are not yet grown. She feels bad that soon they will have no mother.

Giuseppe and Concetta feel that the children must know that she is gravely ill. So that night after supper, as always, the family enters the parlor. Giuseppe and Concetta tell them some of what the doctor said, but Concetta doesn't want them to know that she is dying.

They just tell them that Concetta is sick, and that she may need a little more help with her chores. She does not want to scare the children. The younger children really don't understand, but Mike and Anne know that their mother is not well.

Concetta goes on with her routine of singing. I notice, that there is a slight crackle in Concetta's voice as she looks lovingly at her children. Giuseppe wipes a tear away from his face as she sings.

The family continue their regular routine for a short time.

Frank, Antonetta and Vincenzo visit. Concetta sings in the parlor a few more times. I watch as she plays her harmonica and sings for the last time. Her voice is still beautiful, but she is becoming weaker by the days. As Concetta's health continues to weaken, Giuseppe has no choice but to tell the children their mother will not get better. She is going to die.

Concetta explains as the children gather around to listen, "God puts us on this earth like a candle burning. We all start out with a tall candle and when our candle burns down, it's our time to meet him in heaven. Some candles burn faster than others. My candle is one of those. I don't know why, maybe he has another plan for me. Soon I will leave this earth, but my heart will always be with each and everyone of you."

Nancy the youngest says, "But Mama we don't want you to go."

Concetta cries, "Oh sweetheart I know, I don't want to go either, but God wants me."

Everyone is crying and they all walk to their mother and hug her.

"We love you Mama what will we do without you?" cries Anne.

Concetta replies, "You will go on with your life, grow up and have families of your own, and I will be with you in spirit. Anne you are my oldest daughter. I am going to leave you in charge to help take care of your brothers and sisters. Make sure you feed them, get them off to school on time, and don't forget church. When you are feeling down, say the rosary and pray to Mary."

The sadness overwhelms everyone. Then Concetta tells Anne, "You hold on to Frank. He is a good boy Anne. Mike, you and your brothers help your father. Your father will need all the help he can get."

Then she looks at everyone and says, "Don't forget, before bed at night, say your prayers and I will always be there praying with you."

Giuseppe tells Concetta, "I wonder why things happen the way they do. Everything I have done through the years, I have done for you and the children. I couldn't wait for you to come from the other side so we could have a life here in Madison. I don't understand why God would take you away from me and the children. Did we do something wrong? I always thought that we would grow old together."

"Oh Giuseppe I'm so sorry," Concetta says as she cries softly.

A few days later Concetta becomes very sick and is put into the hospital for a time, but the doctors say there is nothing that they can do for her. She is sent home and soon there after, she becomes bed-ridden. This is a very difficult time for the family. Giuseppe has to work even more to pay the hospital bills and this means less time for him to be with Concetta. Anne is forced to stop school at seventeen years old to take care of her mother, get her brothers and sisters off to school, clean the house and cook for everyone. It is a very hard life for Anne. There's not much leisure time for her. Frank visits often and helps Anne when he can. Antonetta cooks for the family two or three times a week.

Just as the doctor predicted Concetta's health slowly deteriorates. In the evenings after supper instead of going to the parlor, everyone goes into Concetta's bedroom where they have put their victrola, so she can hear the Italian songs that she loves so much.

Concetta gradually gets to the point where she spends hours moaning in pain. Anne is by her side most of the time and is responsible for giving her mother morphine shots for the pain.

It is nearing Christmas and Concetta takes a turn for the worst slipping in and out of consciousness. There will be no Christmas for the family this year.

Giuseppe tells everyone, "If Concetta can't have a good time then we can't either."

Antonetta knows that Anne has been working very hard, so she makes the family a Christmas dinner and takes it to their house.

In the early morning hours of December 29, 1932, Concetta slips into a comma. The family summons Monsignor Danhaur from Saint

Vincent's. He is a good friend of the family. When he comes into the room, he senses that Concetta is close to death. He asks the family to come into the bedroom to say the rosary with him. They circle around Concetta's bed and begin to pray. About half way through the rosary, at 10:30 in the morning, Concetta dies peacefully in her sleep, with everyone she loves at her side. She was 49 years old and had been sick for about a year.

Within seconds of her death, the smell of roses enters the room.

This seems odd because there are no roses in the house, and it's late December with snow and ice everywhere. I am able to see her spirit separating from her body! She gently floats over the top of her bed and looks down at her family as they grieve. She no longer looks like the sickly woman that laid dying in that bed just a few seconds before. She stays for a few minutes, walks and stands behind Anne, and gently puts her hand on Anne's shoulder. Anne closes her eyes as though she feels a warm sensation enter her mind and body. It's as though Concetta is giving her strength and power. She knows that Anne will need this to carry on. Surprisingly, I am the only one that can see Concetta, and I wonder what kind of world I am in, where I am able to see both the living, the dead and the past! Concetta then takes her hand from Anne's shoulder, and drifts to the top of her bed and disappears.

From that day forward, as a tribute to her mother Anne attends the 8:00 A.M. mass every morning after everyone goes off to school and work. Then she would go home and do what Concetta had instructed her to do before she passed away. Everyone misses their mother. They miss going into the parlor at night, they miss her beautiful singing voice and they miss her when they say their prayers at night. The family is strong and I believe that Concetta's spirit is really close by, when every now and then, the smell of roses is in the air. I knew that Giuseppe grew roses and you could smell them when they were in bloom, but what about winter when there were no roses? Anne's faith and prayers keep her strong. She too senses her mother's presence as the smell of roses enters the home.

Chapter Seven

The Adoption

In 1933, Frank tells his parents that he would like to ask Anne to marry him. They love Anne because she comes from a good Italian family. She has worked hard taking care of her father, brothers, and sisters since her mother's death.

Once they give their approval, Vincenzo and Antonetta realize they need to talk to Frank. They ask him to go outside with them to their favorite spot under the apple trees. Frank senses that something is suspicious. As I observe, I believe that this conversation will reveal a secret that Vincenzo and Antonetta have been hiding from Frank for many years.

Both Vincenzo and Antonetta have a strained look on their faces.

Frank has never really seen them like this.

Frank asks, "What's wrong? You don't seem happy."

Antonetta replies, "Frank we are happy for you, we love Anne and we want you to marry her, and we want her for our daughter in-law."

For a moment there is a silence as Antonetta looks at Vincenzo as if to say help me.

Vincenzo never had a hard time getting to the point, but it is obvious that what ever he is going to say, isn't going to be easy.

Then Vincenzo says. "Frank there is something you need to know about yourself." Stuttering, Vincenzo says in Italian, "We... We never told you this because we loved you and we didn't want you to leave us.

There is no easy way of telling you this, so I'm just going to try to explain this the best I know how. Frank, when you were a baby, you were put into an adoption home in New York City. Your mother and I could not have children and we wanted a child to carry on our name. We went to talk to the priest at Saint Vincent's, he told us about an orphanage run by Catholic nuns. It was a New York foundling home. You were about three years old at the time. There were a lot of other babies that we looked at there, but as soon as we saw you, we knew you had to come home with us. You were in a crib, you seemed like you were the skinniest baby there and you kept pulling on my sleeve and looking at us, as if to say please take me home with you. We loved you from the moment we saw you."

Vincenzo pauses for a moment to let all of this sink in. Frank sits quietly under the apple trees. He isn't sure what to think. I can see that he is confused.

Finally, Frank asks, "Why didn't you tell me this before?"

Antonetta meekly replies, "Because Frank, we were afraid you would leave us and go look for your real parents."

"What's my real name, is it Frank?"

Vincenzo replies, "On the certificate we have, it says your real name is Edwin O'Connor and you were born on October 12, 1905."

Vincenzo hands him the certificate from the orphanage. Frank's mind is going a mile a minute as he reads it. He isn't sure what to ask next.

"Who is my mother, my father?" Frank asks in a dazed-like state.

Vincenzo says, "They said that your mother got into some kind of trouble and left you there with the sisters. We don't know anything else about your parents. They didn't seem to know anything at the foundling either, or at least that's what they lead us to believe.

There was no mention about your father at all."

"Do you know where I was born?" Frank asked.

"You were born someplace in New York," Vincenzo replied.

Frank is confused, I can see that he feels alone. Then he says, "I wonder who I really am, and where I really came from?"

"Frank," Antonetta said. "We love you no matter who you are or where you came from. We never thought of you as anything else but our son. Your a good boy and a good son."

Vincenzo and Antonetta look at each other, as they both feel an emptiness. They wonder if they had done the right thing by keeping this a secret from him all these years.

Frank gets up from his bench, he tells his parents, "I'm going for a walk to the Spring Garden. I'll be back soon."

This is the first time I see him go into the woods without traps or a hunting rifle. He needs to be alone to think, and his parents understand this. I watch as he walks down the old road and into the woods. At this moment, I begin to realize how lost my father feels and how lost his spirit was on the day he died. He wants to know who his mother is and why she left him.

Frank finds a quiet spot to sit down. As he watches the water trickling in the gentle stream, he pictures in his mind all the good times he spent with Vincenzo as a boy in these woods hunting and trapping. As he continues sitting there in thought, out of nowhere comes a little dog that looks like his beloved friend Bocce. He runs up to him wagging his tail and licking him on the face and then sits next to him.

Frank looks at him and says, "Where did you come from little friend? You look just like a dog I had once."

The little dog gets as close to Frank as he can get. He looks up at him with those innocent eyes. This cheers Frank up.

Then Frank gets up and begins to walk and the little dog follows.

They walk to the old clock tower and climb to the top, as he and Bocce had done so many times in the past. As they stare at the New York skyline, Frank tries to imagine what his biological mother looks like and why she wasn't able to keep him. He also realizes how much his parents are a part of his life. The little dog barks at Frank like Bocce used to do, as if to say it's time to go back home to his parents. They head back down the tower and walk back to the old homestead. When Frank reaches the front yard, he turns and the little dog is no longer with him. Frank then realizes that the little dog was Bocce, and he was trying to help him remember all the good times they had growing up.

Vincenzo and Antonetta are sitting on the front porch waiting.

Neither of them says a word, as they wonder what Frank is thinking.

Frank breaks the silence by saying, "I have been thinking all afternoon, I love you both no matter what. In my eyes this doesn't change our relationship, You will always be my parents. You brought me up, you fed me and I hunted and trapped with you pop and you both gave me a roof over my head. But there is one thing I would like to do. I would like to go to this foundling home. I am curious to see what it looks like. Maybe they will be able to tell me something about why I was left there. I promise I'll be back. I still want to marry Anne."

They are happy with Frank's decision.

Vincenzo says, "Frank there is one more thing. We are your foster parents; we never legally adopted you. If you want your name to be Frank Sapio when you marry Anne, we will have to get a lawyer to draw up the papers to change your name. It's your choice, we love you no matter what your name is."

Frank pauses and then says, "No, I have always been Frank Sapio and I don't want that to change. I'm proud of the name you gave me.

Another name just wouldn't feel right."

Frank can tell that his reply makes Vincenzo very proud. After all, Frank knew that this was what his parents wanted. After their conversation, Frank goes directly over to Anne's to tell her what he has just found out and also to ask for her hand in marriage.

He says, "I want to visit this foundling home. I would like to see where I lived for the first three years of my life."

But deep in his heart he is also hoping that someone there will be able to shed some light on who his mother was, and maybe someone there will be able to help him find her.

"Anne the real reason I came over, was to ask you if you will marry me. I want to take care of you and be with you forever. Will you marry me Anne?"

Anne thinks of her mother for a second and what she had told her about Frank. Then with tears of joy, accepts.

Frank tells Anne to begin making plans. He tells her, "I should not be gone for more than three or four days. Once I get this off my chest we can get on with our lives."

Frank doesn't want to upset his parents, so he doesn't say too much about what he is going to do. He promises them that his relationship with them will never change, no matter what he finds out in New York. They understand and know what he has to do. They just hope that he will return.

The next morning Frank goes to the Madison train station and purchases a ticket for himself. As a boy, he remembered the train tracks when they were level with the road and the gateman sitting in his little shack. He would watch the train as it came through Madison and dream of riding it someday. By now the tracks have been raised and a brand new Gothic style station has been built. Only twenty-four miles from New York's Manhattan Island, many people now commute to the city to work. To get away from the hustle and bustle of the city, Madison and the surrounding country side is the ideal place to live.

When he gets to the city, it's overwhelming. It's so much different than Madison. He remembered looking at the city from the top of the clock tower at the Ward's estate. It looked so peaceful from there. Now it is a bit intimidating. The streets are packed with people hustling to get somewhere. Everybody seems to be in a hurry. There are peddlers pushing fruit carts and paper boys yelling the headlines. He needs to ask for directions. It couldn't be that hard to ask a stranger. But unlike Madison, these people are not willing to take time out of their busy lives for anyone. Frustrated, he sees that most of the people are waving down a taxi. He decides that this is the best thing to do. He tells the driver where he wants to go and the driver knows immediately where it is located. Within a few minutes we pull up in front of the foundling. A chill goes down my father's spine as he looks out the window and pays the cabby.

He stands outside the foundling and tries to gather his composure. He is elated and at the same time sad, as he closes his eyes and tries to imagine what his mother was feeling and thinking when she gave him away. He tries to imagine what she looked like, but he can't.

He opens his eyes and scans the crowd walking by. He is subconsciously looking for someone, anyone who might be his mother. He wishes so much that she will come out of the building and greet him, but she doesn't.

As I watch, I can feel his heartache. So he gathers his emotions and proceeds to walk inside.

Although improved, It remained much like I remembered when I was last here back in 1908. There are children, nurses, and nuns everywhere.

A sister senses that Frank is puzzled and says, "Can I help you?"

"Yes Sister," he replies. "My name is Frank Sapio and I was taken from here almost twenty-five years ago and raised by foster parents. I just found out last week that this is where I was as a baby. I was wondering if you have any records of my mother. She named me Edwin O'Connor. I'm getting married soon and before I start a family, I want to find out who I am and where I came from."

The sister sympathetically looks him in the eye; he can tell that he isn't the first to ask for this kind of information.

"I'm sorry, it's against the law for us to give out any information about the children that are taken from here or anything regarding their background. I really wish that I could help you," the sister replied.

"Please Sister, what will it hurt, I just want to know why my mother gave me up!"

The sister says, "I'm sorry I can't help you. We see people like you every so often inquiring about the same thing, but we have to turn them away. A lot of the mothers that leave their children here do not want any further contact with them. I don't know if yours is a case such as this. There are so many reasons why children are left here.

But no matter what the case circumstances are, we have to treat everyone the same. I'm sorry but the records are sealed."

I can see tears well up in my father's eyes. He is desperate, "I just want to know who my mother is. Can't you just tell me that much Sister? I feel like she would want me to know."

"I'm sorry sir, but I just can't. Like I said the records are sealed."

With that comment Frank slowly turns around and walks out the door. As he is leaving, he almost runs into a young woman holding her baby. She seems confused as to whether or not she should go in. Finally she does. Frank turns around and follows her inside. She tells the sister that she is poor and can not support another child. He wonders if this is why his mother left him so many years ago.

Disappointed, he leaves once again. It's time for him to go back to Madison. He needs to try to get on with his life. As he rides the train, he is thinking that his trip wasn't in vain. At least he got to see where he was as a baby, and he walked on the same floors as his mother, Vincenzo, and Antonetta once did years ago. But he would always wonder who his mother was and the reason she left him there.

When he returns home his parents are waiting. They ask him how it went. He tells them that they wouldn't give him any information.

Vincenzo says, "While you were in New York, I went to see the lawyer. He said we need to go to the courthouse with him so we can adopt you and make your name legal."

On September 22, 1933, a formal adoption takes place at the Morris County Orphans' Court. It is an emotional moment as Frank signs the papers that will officially change his name forever. This will be the first and last time that he would ever sign his birth name. This very private moment makes the local paper.

27 Year Old Adopted In Unusual Case

After living with Mr. and Mrs. Vincenzo Sapio of Greenwood Avenue for twenty-five years, Edwin O'Connor was formally adopted by them on Friday afternoon. His name was changed from Edwin O'Connor to Frank Sapio.

In 1908, Mr. and Mrs. Sapio took him home when he was only three years old to serve as his foster parents. Frank is now twenty-seven years old, and his new parents are fifty-two and forty-five. Under law, adopted parents must be fifteen years older than the person being adopted. Frank is the second adult to be adopted in Morris County since the law was passed in 1925 permitting such action. Judge Allen Hall presided in Orphans' Court to confirm the adoption.

The Sapio's picked up their son from a New York foundling home and brought him to Madison, where they have lived for most of their lives. Although his birth name is Edwin, he has always been called Frank. He was educated at Saint Vincent's School in Madison. When asked why the formal adoption was made so many years later, the Sapio's explained that Frank plans to marry a Madison girl and wished to do so under his foster parents' name.

On a lovely summer day of July 14, 1934, Frank and Anne are married. It's a beautifully celebrated High Mass. Anne walks proudly down the long aisle of Saint Vincent's Church with her father Giuseppe at her side. She looks beautiful in her stunning Saks Fifth Avenue wedding gown, with an extra long train that seems as though it reaches the back of the church, her hair is pulled back and she is wearing a white veil complimented by a bouquet of freshly cut white orchids, baby's breath and lilies of the valley. Giuseppe lifts Anne's veil and they hug. She watches him take his seat, I see a bit of sadness in Anne's eyes as she watches him. There is an empty space next to Giuseppe, where Concetta would have been sitting. I know, that she wishes her mother were here for this very special occasion.

She remembers what her mother told the family before she passed away. "She said that she would always be with them in spirit."

As they begin to take their vows, I glance over and next to Giuseppe is Concetta, she looks like an angel, watching over her family.

Again, I'm bewildered by my power that I am able to see the spirit world. The weather co-operates and a huge Italian garden reception is held at the old homestead. The reception is everything anyone would want; there's all kinds of food, wine, lemonade and punch and of course the traditional playing of bocce ball. The yard is decorated with streamers, confetti, and freshly cut orchids and baby's breath at every table compliments of Anne's father, Giuseppe. The yard enhances the celebration with its natural beauty. The main table is set in front of these pink and white giant hydrangea bushes, which are in full bloom. There is a band playing music, and when they go off to take their breaks, an Italian tenor sings old Italian love songs to the couple.

Anne tells Frank, "I wish my mother were here for this, she would have been so pleased."

And I wished, that I were able to tell Anne that she is here.

I stand there watching as all the old men walk up to the couple and hand them their envelopes. Italians are big on envelopes!

Taking in the sights, sounds and smells of this event, it is surreal to see my parents get married.

For their honeymoon, they drive to Canada. Appropriately, Frank drives the same car he drove on their first date. Neither one of them has ever been out of Madison, with the exception of my father's one time trip to New York to visit the foundling home. I can see their excitement as they take in the sights along the way. They stay for about two weeks near Niagara Falls, a honeymoon paradise for this period of time. But it is time to go on with their lives as husband and wife so they head back to Madison.

Although he is content and happy with Anne, Frank still can't get his mother out of his head. He wants to know who she is, what she looked like, and why she gave him away. He realizes, though, that he has to get on with his life; he has a wife to support. He continues to go hunting and trapping with his father, as this has been a way of life for them ever since they can remember. They do very well selling pelts.

When he can, Frank also helps his father around the farm before and after work.

Vincenzo told Frank that when he married Anne, they could live down the street in the 1850 farm house. Both Frank and his father had done a lot of work on it through the years. It is still the only house in sight with woods and a cornfield surrounding it. The Spring Garden and the Rosedale Woods, that Frank used to frequent as a boy and where he hunts with his father, is right across the street.

Vincenzo is generous enough to let the young couple get settled first, and when they are able to afford it, they can pay rent. Frank doesn't believe in handouts, and as soon as he gets his first pay check, he pays his rent to his father. The newlyweds are up everyday at 5:00 a.m. Like she promised her mother, Anne is busy everyday taking care of her brothers, sisters and her father. They live about a mile away. After Frank leaves for work, Anne walks to her old house on Walnut Street, hurries with her chores, and is still able to make the 8:00 a.m. mass at Saint Vincent's. She Then goes back home to take care of her own chores.

On July 22, 1935, Frank and Anne's first son is born. They are so excited and happy. This little boy is to be named Jimmy. They name him after Vincenzo, which surprisingly can mean both James or Vincent when translated into English, at least that's what I was always told. It is Italian tradition to always name the first son after the grandfather on his father's side. This makes Vincenzo very proud.

Even with the birth of her new son, my mother keeps her promise to her mother, no matter what the weather, Anne continues to help her family.

The years pass and the family continues to grow. Two more children are born, both are girls, Bevy and Linda. Frank wants his children to have brothers and sisters. He doesn't want them to grow up alone like he did.

By this time Anne's sisters are old enough to cook and take care of their father and the house. After so many years of keeping her promise to Concetta, Anne is able to focus all of her attention on her own family.

Vincenzo continues to work on the different estates around Madison. One day while working on the Green's estate, Mr. Green approaches Vincenzo. He knows that Vincenzo has always been a hard worker and he respects Vincenzo for that. He asks him if he would like to stay on and work permanent for a weekly salary. No one has ever offered Vincenzo a deal like this. For most of his life, he has always worked from day to day. This makes him very happy. He accepts and shows up everyday for work for the next few years, never missing a day.

Vincenzo and Antonetta are content. Frank stays close to his parents and continues to help them in anyway that he can. He still visits every morning before and after work like he has done for years.

Vincenzo still uses a horse and buggy to get to where he needs to go.

Him and cars never did work out. Frank never offered to teach him again, and Vincenzo never showed an interest.

The year is 1947, Vincenzo gets up to go to work as usual. He and Antonetta are sitting in the kitchen talking. He sits down to have his morning coffee, when all of a sudden, he drops his coffee cup and it crashes to the floor. Antonetta gets up to pick up the broken glass and as she does, Vincenzo falls from his chair to the floor. She realizes that Vincenzo is not moving. Antonetta tries to help him up, but she can't.

Vincenzo says, "Antonetta, I can't move, something is wrong with my legs! I can't move them!"

Just then Frank walks in, he sees his father laying on the floor and Antonetta struggling trying to help him up.

"Ma, what happened?" Frank asks.

"He was sitting here drinking his morning coffee, when he dropped it and he fell on the floor. I've been trying to help him up, but he is too heavy. Something is wrong with him Frank, he can't get up!"

In Italian Frank asks, "Pop, what's the matter, why can't you get up?"

Vincenzo Replies, "Something is wrong with my legs, I've got to get up, I'm going to be late for work!"

His father has always been an extremely tough man, so it is difficult to imagine him being so helpless. Frank immediately rings the operator and asks her to call the doctor. When he arrives at the house and sees my grandfather he knows what has happened. He examines Vincenzo. Then he asks Frank and Antonetta to help him move

Vincenzo to the bed and tells them to wait in the kitchen. After about ten minutes, the doctor returns. Antonetta is sitting in her chair at the kitchen table, and Frank is looking out the window.

He says, "Vincenzo has had a stroke, he appears to have very little feeling or control in his legs. As it is right now he is unable to walk. You can try to help him move his legs and sometimes the feeling will come back, but in this case due to the severity of the stroke, I don't think that this will happen. He will probably never walk again. I'll come back and check on him later this afternoon. In the meantime he needs to stay in bed and rest. Sometimes another stroke can occur within twenty-four hours of the first one. Don't let him get excited about anything. Keep a close watch on him."

They are saddened by the news that Vincenzo may never walk again.

Antonetta suddenly feels frighten. "I don't know how I'm going to do it Frank," she says.

"Ma, we will work it out, I will help you," Frank replies.

Antonetta goes into the bedroom and sits with Vincenzo as he sleeps.

Frank returns home to tell Anne what has happened. He tells her that he is going to have to help his mother as much as possible. She understands because she has been through all of this before with her own family.

Frank returns to the old homestead. Antonetta is still at Vincenzo's side. He sits with his mother for the rest of the afternoon waiting for the doctor's return. Shortly there after, Anne comes over with the three children and plates of food for the family. When the doctor returns, he re-examines Vincenzo only to confirm what he had said to them earlier in the day. By now Vincenzo has lost all of the feeling in his legs, he will never walk again.

All Vincenzo is worried about, is that he is going to be late for work at Mr. Green's place. He thinks that his condition is only temporary and that this will pass, and that he will be better by morning. Little does he know that he will never walk again.

Frank tells Mr. Green about what happened.

"The doctor told us that my father is never going to be able to walk again, he is paralyzed from the waist down. All pop is worried about is being late for work."

Later that day, Mr. Green pays Vincenzo a visit. He tells Vincenzo not to worry about anything. He tells him his health comes first.

Vincenzo feels like he has let everyone down. He tells Mr. Green that as soon as he gets better he will be back.

Antonetta is in the kitchen cooking. After visiting with Vincenzo for a while, Mr. Green walks into the kitchen. Antonetta asks him to stay for supper. She tells him that Frank should be here soon. He accepts. She thanks him for coming over, and that Vincenzo is happy that he came by. Mr. Green is more like a friend than an employer to Vincenzo.

Antonetta waits on her husband hand and foot. She takes his supper to him in bed. While she is feeding him Frank arrives. Mr. Green is finally able to get Antonetta and Frank alone, away from Vincenzo. I could tell that his stay was leading up to something. The three of them sit down to eat together.

Mr. Green tells them, "Vincenzo has always been my number one man, he has taken care of my place as though it were his own. I have never had to tell him what to do. He has never missed a day of work since I put him on salary. He is a good man. This morning, before I came over here, I walked around the estate and I was thinking, everything on the property looks so nice and it's all because of Vincenzo. I look at the apple orchard and I think of how Vincenzo grafted the trees to get two different types of apples on one tree. All of the stonework, Vincenzo did. I would like to continue to pay Vincenzo his salary until he gets better."

Mr. Green knows that Vincenzo is not going to get better.

Frank and his mother are taken completely by surprise. They don't know what to say.

"Mr. Green, that is so nice of you. I know my father always liked you a lot," Frank said.

Mr. Green replies, "I feel like I want to help you in anyway that I can, I feel that Vincenzo deserves it."

On August 30, 1947, I was born. My birth brings a mixture of emotions. Frank and Anne are excited, but at times it's difficult to be happy, because they know Vincenzo can't go on like this forever. On Sunday afternoons my parents bring all of us kids over to visit him. My mother and Antonetta make Sunday dinner, usually macaroni and meat balls. When the weather is nice, my brother and sisters play outside or help my father in the garden. By now the farm animals have dwindled away. Just a few chickens linger in the yard, and only two dogs remain.

A fox terrier named Spot, and a black cocker spaniel named Nicky.

On March 7,1948, Vincenzo's condition worsens. My father takes me to visit him.

As I lay on the bed next to Vincenzo, he whispers in my ear, "You need to live now, and it's my time to die."

It was strange hearing him say those words to me. I could never understand what those words meant then, because I was just a baby, but now I understood what he meant. It was time for him to move on.

The next night, on March 8,1948, at 11:30 p.m. Vincenzo dies peacefully in his sleep. He was only sixty-seven years old. Mr. Green did continue to pay him his salary until the day he died. He also paid for all of the funeral expenses.

His body is laid out in the living room for people to view. As in Italian tradition, my father stays and guards the body each night after everyone leaves until the day of the funeral. I can tell my father has lost a best friend. They did everything together. He will be missed. I can sympathetically relate to that moment as it was the same feeling that I had when my father died.

Chapter Eight

The Colors Of A Pheasant

In spite of Vincenzo's death my father continues his way of life.

He hunts, traps, and walks in the woods. In summer he takes us to the woods to pick blackberries and my mother makes jam from what we bring home. Frank has a love of nature, and he is an expert in identifying all of the animals' tracks. He takes us to the Spring Garden for walks.

He tells us that the raccoon's foot print looks like a persons hand. He shows us where the muskrats play at night and where they would slide down the banks to get into the water. Some of the trees have their bark missing, this is where a buck has been rubbing his antlers. He tells us to watch the squirrels as they gather their nuts and hide them for winter. He shows us the colors of a pheasant, and tells us to listen and watch the sky in late fall for the Canadian geese flying south.

This is a sure sign that winter is not far away. He shows us where he and his father walked and rested. Then he shares a bit of history as he tells us that before us, Indians roamed these woods. Our walks are treasured, especially since we know that he used to walk these same woods with his father. Just smelling the pine and hearing the wind rustle the leaves, brings back many memories.

When I was a boy, he would take me to his special spot; the old clock tower. The estate had been turned into a golf course, but the old clock tower still remained standing tall. It was the only thing left of the Ward's estate. We would climb the spiral staircase to the top. I gasped at the sight of the New York skyline which had grown considerably since my father was a boy. I always sensed a loneliness about my father like there was something missing in his life. Often when we would look at the skyline he would express his desire to find out about his mother. He pictured her walking in the streets of New York, alone and pregnant. He felt she must have been forced to give him up.

He had a strong desire for the family to know that he was adopted and how his mother left him at the foundling. Because my father spoke of her so often, we felt as though we should know her.

As I watch us talking about his mother, I realize now, that maybe he was pleading for me back then to help find her. As a boy I couldn't have picked up on this. But now I do and this realization makes me more compelled than ever to find her.

By 1954, my parents have saved enough money to build a house.

Antonetta gives my parents permission to build on the property right across the street from the old homestead in the cornfield. After Vincenzo died corn was no longer planted on this piece of property.

There were a few apple and pear trees but nothing else. My father continues to visit Antonetta everyday and we still plant a garden at the old homestead. Antonetta misses Vincenzo and talks of him as though he is still here.

Within a few months the builders clear the property and start to build. Anxiously my parents are there everyday to check the progress.

It takes about five months to complete. In 1955, we move into the new house. My mother's father Giuseppe comes over a couple of times a week and helps my father landscape. He plants evergreens, dogwood trees and white birch trees. They put in a split rail fence that surrounds the property lines and at every post Giuseppe plants climbing roses which brighten everything up. I love living here, and I love living across the street from my grandmother. A couple of years before, my father had suggested that she move upstairs and rent the bottom half out for extra income. I visit her almost everyday in summer. I love to explore and play in the old barns.

By now all of the farm animals are gone. The brick house is still here, but it isn't the same as when Vincenzo was alive. It's sad to see the barrels of wine had turned to vinegar.

Along with my brother, father and Antonetta we all help in the greenhouse and garden. This is the one tradition that we continue to carry on. My father and Antonetta insist that there is nothing better than freshly grown vegetables, especially ours.

Sometimes on summer weekends we all go to Lake Hopatcong, which is about thirty miles northwest of Madison. My mother packs a big picnic basket, we all swim for a while and eat lunch. My mother always said that we needed to stay out of the water for at least an hour after lunch or else we could get cramps and drown. Later in the day we head for the famous amusement park, Bertrand Island. Its been around since the 1880s. I love the old rickety roller coaster, but my father never trusts it, he can't wait to get off. He likes the shooting gallery.

He tells us that the sights are purposely off on the guns. In spite of this trickery my father wins anyway. We know he is a good shot.

On long holiday weekends, we get up 4:30 in the morning and head for Atlantic City. It's a long drive, over a hundred miles from Madison. We swim for most of the day. When our lips turn purple my mother makes us get out of the water and sit under the umbrella. In spite of this, we all get sunburned anyway. Later that day we stroll down the boardwalk to look at all of the amusements and get something to eat. I love the foot long hot-dogs. We've never seen so many people and so much excitement. The side streets are lined with these large elegant looking homes that are right next to one another, and within walking distance to the ocean and the amusements. Since there aren't too many hotels, families rent rooms in these homes, where maybe four or five other families are staying. This is where we stay. The hardest thing about this is there is only one bathroom out in the hallway for all of the families to share. One has to wait their turn to get in, and most of the time there is a long line.

At night we head for the great "Steel Pier" and watch the famous diving horse with a rider, usually a girl, as they stand at the edge of a large platform and jump into the ocean. I feel sorry for the horse.

I'm not sure if he has much of a choice, but on the other hand maybe he is enjoying himself. We have a great time and the weekend seems to go by really fast. The ride home feels like it is taking forever, as we have such blistering sunburns, and there is no air conditioning in the car. I can't even sit back against the seat or let anyone rub up against me, because my sunburn is so bad. I think I have sun poison. It even hurts to wear a shirt.

Both my parents enjoy the holidays. Thanksgiving and Christmas are our favorites. On Thanksgiving, the entire family dresses in our finest clothes. We all sit at the dining room table, which faces a giant picture window. We say a prayer of thanks, and pray for those who can't be here. Just as we are about to eat, snow flakes begin to fall.

As I get up to look, I hear the familiar sound of Canadian geese honking as they fly over the house. My father reminds us that winter is right around the corner.

Christmas is everyone's favorite. Our traditional meal for Christmas Eve is spaghetti, shrimp, and salted cod. My father goes to the fish market to pick up the cod three or four days before Christmas Eve. The cod needs to be soaked in water, changing the water everyday for a few days before cooking to remove the salt. And then there's the eel, I don't know why, but they need to be killed the same day that they are going to be eaten. So there are two trips to the market. But he enjoys it. The fish market is packed with Italians, all the old timers speak in Italian. I feel like I'm in Italy as I stand there watching my father speaking in Italian. He doesn't look Italian because of his brilliant blue eyes and light complexion. But growing up with Vincenzo and Antonetta, he thinks and feels Italian. This confuses those who don't know my father because he is so fluent in the language.

After Christmas Eve dinner, my father calls our cousins at their house and places a towel over his mouth, pretending to be Santa Claus, he asks if they have been good.

He tells them that he is ahead of schedule and very close to Madison and that they should go to bed, so he can deliver their gifts. To keep the spirit of Santa, it isn't unusual for my father to get up in the middle of the night in a snow storm, go outside with an old set of sleigh bells, hide in the woods next to the house and jingle the bells. I never would have thought that it was anyone else out there in the woods but Santa! Our mother and father keep our imaginations alive.

On Christmas day we are going to the 10:00 a.m. mass at Saint Vincent's. After church, we visit my godfather. He is an undertaker who owns and operates the Madison Funeral Parlor and he lives upstairs from where the bodies are laid out. I'm always a little scared of going there because to get where he lives, we have to go through the downstairs where the bodies are. I can't wait to get upstairs. I stay close to my parents' side. We have a drink usually a shot or two of Anisette. My mother reminds me to sip it slow. The whole time that we are visiting, I'm wishing that there was another way out of here. He gives me a gift and they talk a while. They ask how everyone is and discuss those who have died. He tells me, when I am old enough, I can come to work for him. I can start out as a doorman or usher. Little does he know, that I can't wait to get to the car in the parking lot.

When we leave we take a ride to the cemetery where all of the relatives are buried and if the snow is too deep, we stay in the car and just look. Today is one of those days. On our way home, my parents knowing that I was afraid to go there, would tease me and say, "Why don't you become an undertaker." The cemetery didn't bother me.

It was the funeral parlor that I felt uncomfortable in.

When we get home, my father and I walk across the street to visit my grandmother, Antonetta. We take her a gift, usually an apron. I never remember her not wearing an apron. We walk upstairs, she is sitting at the kitchen table looking out the window. She seems lonely.

"Merry Christmas ma! Merry Christmas grandma!"

Then she laughs and says, "Merry Christmas honey, but it's just another day."

And again she talks about her husband and how he was drinking his coffee when he had his stroke. I listen to her, she really misses him.

My father says, "Why don't you come over later ma, everybody is going to be there."

She replies, "I can't stay long, I'm in bed at 7:00 o'clock."

We walk back across the street and as we come in through the cellar door, the house smells of my mother's good cooking, and the sound of Mario Lanza Christmas records playing in the background. Later in the day, all of the relatives come over. Everyone brings a covered dish. My father and I walk across the street to get my grandmother.

My grandfather Giuseppe rides with one of my aunts or uncles.

Someone always brings a movie camera with the lights that are so hot and bright, they make you sweat and go blind for a few seconds. After dinner, we watch home movies from the previous Christmas's. The night ends with everyone singing carols while my sister plays the piano. It feels odd watching all of the people when they were young, and even stranger still, to see the ones who have died sitting and talking to one another. It was always such a joyous time.

After everyone is gone and just before bed, my mother puts Mario Lanza's last song on the record player called, "Guardian Angels." It's sad but it lulls everyone to sleep.

Guardian angels around my bed. Guarding me in my prayer, they hush the shadows when they dance about, they shoo away the bad. Guardian angels to comfort me if I wake in the night. They gather all my dreams, their halo's are my light, they dry my tears if I should weep, they tuck me in, they rouse me from my dreams. Guardian angels around my bed, standing by until I rise, there's one with shining angel's wings, who shows me paradise.

Chapter Nine

Your Mother's Name

It's 1959 and Giuseppe's health is deteriorating. He feels weak and tired. His roses and raking the stones in his manicured garden are neglected due to his weakness. Even though he doesn't want to go, the family insists that he see a doctor. The diagnosis is quick and clear, he has colon cancer and there is no cure. He still works outside as much as he can, and when he is tired he rests in the shade under a pear tree. The pears are ripe and Giuseppe takes out his pocket knife, peels a pear, and shares it with the children.

Poor Giuseppe, I can tell he is in pain, but he never complains.

He loves raking the stones, It seems as though it is a therapy for him. He rakes and rakes and rakes, over and over until not one stone is out of place. Soon he is no longer able to tend to his roses or his stones. I can see the pain in his face. The rose garden seems to be lonely without him there. The roses begin to droop and look sad. On March 6, 1959, with family at his bedside Giuseppe dies. He was seventy-five years old. Minutes before his death, The smell of roses enters the room. As I stand there watching, I see Concetta. She is holding her hand out for him. She tells him that she has been waiting for him and it's time for him to go. The funeral is big. Everyone that knew him is there. He was well respected and he would be missed. He is laid next to his wife Concetta at Saint Vincent's cemetery. My father begins to wonder more and more about his birth mother. He tells us kids the story over and over of how he thinks his mother left him at the door step of the foundling one morning. He wants so much to know more.

Who was she? What did she look like? Who was his father? So many unanswered questions.

Out of all our grandparents, Antonetta is the only one left. She constantly thinks of her husband Vincenzo. She talks about him frequently. In winter, she wears his clothes. She is a mighty rugged lady, wearing his old black floppy felt hat, with a feather from a pheasant sticking out of the ban above the hat rim, his arctic boots, and his long black button down overcoat. I watch her as she shovels the snow from her path that leads to her coal cellar, where she shovels coal into the furnace to heat the house. She does this a couple of times a day, once in the morning and in the early evening before it gets dark. This heats the house all night and the next morning, she repeats the same routine.

My grandmother never learned to drive and preferred to walk to do her shopping. Every Friday morning she walks to a small Italian store close to the center of town to buy what she needs for the week. She is a very friendly, jovial lady. Everyone in town knows her and offers to give her a ride. Even the garbage man and the coal man offer her rides.

Today I see her get out of the coal truck, dusting the coal dust off of herself that she picked up while riding in the cab.

Not accustomed to modern day amenities, she doesn't own a television set. She doesn't care for one either. But she loves her radio. Standing in her kitchen, I watch her listening to her radio shows. She keeps it on the same station and laughs as she listens to Amos and Andy, and Abbott and Costello. Later in the day my father comes over and asks her if she wants to go see a movie. She has never been to one and is hesitant, but my father insists on treating her. I follow and watch as my father purchases the tickets for a western movie.

They enter the theater and sit down together. Knowing my grandmother like he does, sometimes she talks out loud, so he tells her, "Ma you have to be real quiet in here. You're not supposed to talk."

She is in awe at the size of the screen and wonders about the idea of seeing moving pictures. The movie starts, a gun battle takes place.

She innocently jumps up from her seat and yells, "Frank their shooting at us!"

I knew that bringing my grandmother here was a mistake.

Embarrassed, my father whispers, "Ma, sit down, it's not real!"

They leave the theater early. Poor grandma she didn't mean any harm, she just didn't know any better.

It's snowing tonight and it's freezing outside. My mother a master seamstress, is working hard on her Singer sewing machine. Winter is always a good time to sew as she works for hours making everyone's clothes. My father is reading the paper. Every now and then he gets up and looks out the window in the direction of the old homestead at the snow coming down. I watch, as I know what he is thinking.

Anne turns her attention away from sewing and asks, "Frank, what's the matter? It seems like something is bothering you."

"I'm just thinking about my real mother, I wonder why she didn't keep me. I wonder who I am and where I came from? I wonder if I have another family somewhere? I guess I'll die never knowing why she gave me away."

I see myself as a little boy saying good night and going into my room. As I lay in my bed, from my window, I can see the snow coming down, and the old homestead through the street light in front of the house. It's so peaceful. There is a strange silence except for the sound of the old sewing machine whirring away in the other room, and the distant lonely muffled sound of the train as it comes through Madison.

As the late fifties and early sixties pass, my father begins to become obsessed about his birth mother. It is obvious that not knowing saddens and frustrates him. I catch him looking at strangers, wondering if one of them could be his mother.

He makes several trips to the foundling home in New York, but has no luck. It's the same old story, the law states that records are sealed. Since 1958, the foundling home had moved a couple of times.

Every time it changes location, my father loses a little glimmer of hope.

I watch myself grow up to adolescence. I get a job as a caddie at the golf course where the old clock tower is located. Like my father, I get up early in the morning, hop on my bicycle and leave before the sun comes up. I sneak inside the tower and climb up stairs to look at the New York skyline and the rolling hills around Madison. I would day dream, and think about the stories my father told me about in his childhood, and the circumstances of his being. He wondered what his mother was like.

One day he asked me, "Why do you get up so early in the morning and leave, people don't play golf that early do they?"

I reply, "I go to the clock tower like you did."

He smiles and says, "I haven't been there in a long time."

I can tell that the memories of visiting the clock tower are coming back to him. We stand there in silence. As I stand there watching my dad and me, I notice something that I didn't notice when I was a boy. A tear slowly rolls down his cheek. At that moment, I am more determined to find his mother if it is the last thing I do.

A few more years go by and my brother and sisters marry and start having families of their own. I go off to the military. My parents are alone now. My father visits his mother Antonetta as much as he can. He has converted her house to gas heat now. She hasn't shoveled coal in quite some time. He checks on her everyday and shops for her.

They talk a lot about the old days and how things are different now.

Antonetta continues raking and burning her own leaves as she did in the past. Times have changed. There is an ordinance in Madison now, banning burning.

Frank tells Antonetta, "Ma, there's a law in town your not supposed to burn anymore."

She ignores this and burns anyway. The police come and tell her.

She puts the fire out and as soon as they leave, she starts another fire in another spot. The police come back and she tells them to go talk to her son across the street. Frank explains to the officers that she is old and doesn't understand a lot of the new laws, and that she has been burning for fifty years. Everyone knows Antonetta, even the police.

Frank tells them, "I'll take care of it."

He walks across the street and tells her, "Ma, the police came over and told me we can't burn anymore in Madison. Nobody is allowed to burn. They said to put the leaves in the street, and the town will pick them up."

Antonetta tells Frank, "I always burn my leaves..."

Frank interrupts, thinking he might scare her, and in a kidding tone of voice he says, "Ma, what if they put you in jail?"

She laughs and says, "I don't care they've got to feed me!"

"Ma, they feed you bread!"

Antonetta answers, "I don't care, I like bread!"

Frank tells her, "I'll help you take care of the leaves, let's do it the way the policemen said, so we don't get in trouble."

When they are done working, they walk upstairs and sit at the kitchen table. They have sentimental conversations. She talks about the foundling and remembers so well the day they took Frank home. She tells Frank that there is something that he should know. She tells him that she thinks that his birth mother's name was Hannah and she didn't think that she was married when he was born.

Antonetta still talks of her husband as though his stroke had just happened.

She begins, "He was drinking his morning coffee...I hope God will take me in my sleep. Are you hungry Frank?"

"No ma, I'm not hungry."

Then Frank says, "You were always good to me ma!"

She replies, "We tried the best we knew how."

"I hope I was good to you," Frank said.

"You were always a good boy Frank." Then she changes the subject completely and says, "The taxes are getting so high, I don't know how I'm going to do it!"

My father has been paying the taxes for years, she just doesn't remember.

Then she blurts out the words in broken English, "It'sa not whata you want, It'sa whata you cana do." ("It's not what you want it's what you can do.")

I never fully understood what that meant, but it must have meant something to her.

"Well Ma, I think I better go home now, I'll see you tomorrow."

On his way out the door he turns and says, "Ma, thank you for telling me her name."

Antonetta replies, "That's okay honey be careful crossing the street."

A couple of weeks pass and Antonetta has not gotten up out of bed yet. It's about 8:00 a.m. She is always up at 4:30. Something is wrong!

My father can tell, because he cannot see the reflection of her kitchen light from his house, and my brother who lives down stairs, normally hears her moving around about this time. But today, there is a silence. Although later he did say he heard her talking to someone about 2:00 a.m. He heard her say Vincenzo's name. All of this was true because this time I was here to see it. It's about five minutes before two, Antonetta gets up from what she thinks is a dream. She is disoriented, her heart is racing, and there is a pain in her chest. She sits on the edge of the bed, and there sitting next to her is Vincenzo.

He looks at her and says, "It's time Antonetta."

She lays down and tells him, "I feel tired and weak Vincenzo."

"It's okay Antonetta, I'll help you."

She grips the cruifix in her right hand and holds it to her heart. She closes her eyes and falls asleep. Seconds later, her spirit moves from her body and her and Vincenzo pass through the wall and fade away.

On September 25, 1976, my grandmother Antonetta, in her early nineties passes away. She got her wish and died peacefully in her sleep. She is finally with Vincenzo in heaven.

On their way to the cemetery the procession drives by the old homestead one more time and the hearse carrying Antonetta, momentarily stops in front of her home. My father knew that Antonetta loved the old homestead and stopping here one last time, would have made her very happy.

After her death, my father and brother continue to plant the garden. As time goes on, the barn and the greenhouse start to deteriorate with age. My parents have lots of grandchildren and everyone visits often. He tells them the same stories he told us growing up. He talks about Bocce his best friend.

Then goes on to say, "You know I was a boxer once, I built a ring up in the back near the barn. Everybody from all around used to come to watch the fights. Then one day, this guy by the name of Tommy Bavitt punched me and broke my eardrum. My mother wanted me to quit after that, and I did."

Then he proceeds to get into his boxing stands and punch the air.

All of the kids get such a kick out of this. Then he would play like he was boxing them in slow motion, throwing fake punches. He is quite a character, and most of the time very jolly with his smiling eyes.

Frank no longer hunts, I can see he has grown a soft spot in his heart for the animals. He explains that hunting animals should only be for food. But he loves the woods and shares this love with his grandsons. On weekends he takes them to the river in an old canoe that he had built many years before. When he walks in the woods, he insists that one needs to walk softly so as not to crunch a leaf, as this will scare the animals away. He shows them all the tricks of the woods, and they sit in the same spot as he and his father did many years before.

Chapter Ten

An Old Man's Dreams

As time passes, my parents begin to travel with the church group at Saint Vincent's. Out of their many visits to Europe, Italy and Ireland become their favorite places. In Italy my father is quite comfortable with the locals, as he speaks the language. Both my parents enjoy the people and the history. For my mother though her roots are in Italy. Many times she had wanted to visit her birthplace. Regrettably, the tours they are on never went to the small village where her ancestors came from. She would see Mount Vesuvius, but only from a distance. I know deep in her heart, she wanted to see the house that she lived in as a child. As she would say many times, she remembered sitting near the stone window-sill watching her grandmother walking down the old path towards her house.

Although he speaks and feels Italian my father knows that there is a part of him that is Irish. One day while visiting a very old church in County Mayo, Ireland, as he steps off the bus, he feels a cold chill go down his spine. It grows stronger as he steps through the big iron gates. He breaks away from the tour group. It is a strange feeling and gets stronger as he walks into the church and nears the communion rail. Something or someone is pulling him to stay. Anne comes over and senses something is different, as she knows that Frank is not one to go off by himself. He tells her the sensation; he feels like he knows this place. He doesn't want to leave but the others are beginning to walk to the bus. On his way outside, his attention is taken away from the tour bus as he catches a glimpse of an old cemetery on the side of the church yard and walks towards it.

He tells my mother, "Anne there is something about this place. I don't want to leave. I feel like something happened here that I should know about."

Anne says, "Frank the bus is getting ready to leave we better go."

He is frustrated at having to leave the church and wonders what was drawing him to stay.

When he returns to Madison, he gets back to his routine of working around the house. He plants a few tomatoes, but the garden is not anything like it used to be. Every now and then an old timer, what is left of them, stops by for a while and they talk. My father is one of the few left from this era. He enjoys driving around town in his little Volkswagen and going to the store. On his way home, he stops by the old clock tower. By now it has become too dangerous to climb, as it is falling apart. He sits in his car and stares at the tower. Sadly, this is the last time he sees the tower. It is to be torn down soon.

In his late seventies, he thinks about his mother more and more.

He makes several more trips to the foundling in New York, but it is hard for him to imagine his mother in these streets. It has changed so much.

He also remembers the conversation he had with Antonetta, when she told him she had heard his birth mother's name was Hannah.

Surely, she can't still be alive.

I have been living in Texas for quite sometime now. Both my parents visit as much as they can. March is their favorite time to visit. My father loves planting the garden with me he tells me it reminds him of the old days.

On March 14,1988, my parents come to visit us in Texas, for what will be my fathers final trip. He seems tired and worn. He sits in his favorite chair in my house and tells me of the vivid dreams he has been having.

He says, "Tommy I saw my mother and she was so pretty, she smiled at me. I've been having these dreams a lot, she doesn't say anything, she just smiles at me. She looks like a kind person. I wish I could have known her and I wish I knew where I came from."

I want to help him, but all I can do is listen and say, "I know daddy."

I knew that he had been thinking about her all his life.

They leave Texas after a two week stay. As an observer, I know now that this would be the last time that I would see him alive. He dies six months later. The sadness of this overwhelms me. I can't imagine not knowing who I was or where I came from. My father lived for over eighty years and had never known who he really was. Everyone would really miss him.

#

Suddenly, My sadness is momentarily gone as I am pulled away from my father and whirled back into the present. Shocked, I am sitting in my father's chair! I try to get my bearings as I reflect on everything I had witnessed. My experience was real. I wanted so much to go back. I look at my right hand and I'm still clasping my penny. I know to return I will need to obtain the following years records. To accomplish this, I must know more about my father's mother. Determined, I get up from my chair and begin my quest. I'm thinking if I had my father's original birth certificate it might lead the way. I call my mother and ask her to look around the house to see if it might be there, but she finds nothing. She did tell me that she remembered seeing one a long time ago, but she said that the names of his parents on it were Vincenzo and Antonetta. I didn't think that this one would do me any good. Having hit the first of many obstacles, I go back to the library and research the genealogy section. I ask the librarian if she knows of a place where I might be able to find out how I can get copies of birth certificates from the early 1900s. She refers me to a family history center that had access to public records. When I get there, I tell them that I am searching for my father's roots. I retell the story of how he was taken from a New York foundling in 1908, and that I'm trying to find his birth mother. I explain that I have looked through piles of census records, but I'm really looking for a birth certificate. This would show his place of birth. I dare not share my time travel experience with them, as they will think I'm nuts. Everyone is very eager to help as they all listen to my plight. They can tell by the tone of my voice and the look on my face that I am desperate. Everyone is quite understanding. Knowing that he was born in New York, I know that this is where I need to start looking. Finally, I find a book on New York births and where records were archived for the year 1905. I write them requesting the birth record of Edwin O'Connor, sending it over night mail.

Knowing that he had not been adopted in New York, I write the foundling and inform them that he was taken as a baby from the home and indentured. Through all of my reading and research, I found out that indentured is an agreement for one person to work for another for a certain period of time. I ask them for any records they have. I check the mail box daily. It seems to be taking for ever.

After three weeks pass, I receive an envelope from the archives section in New York City. I know this is it! With trembling hands, I walk inside and open it. At the top in large print, I notice it says Amended Birth Certificate. Everything on it, I already knew except for one thing, the address under his place of birth was on 125th Street in New York City. But this still isn't what I needed. I thought, it's one more piece of the puzzle, and it is better than nothing at all. I know there has to be something else. I began to research more and find out that file numbers on amended birth records always match the numbers on an original birth record, if there was an original.

I write back to them and explain that my father was not adopted when he left the foundling. He was taken and placed with foster parents and indentured and that they sent me the wrong record. I need the original birth record. Could they please check their records to see if they can find a file number that matches the one I have.

Finally after a month goes by, I receive another letter from the archive's department. I tear open the letter. My hopes are high, but I remain a bit cautious so as not to be disappointed. To my disbelief, this was it, the original birth record is enclosed! I read it over and over again, looking for any clues about his mother. The record says, that his mother was from Yorktown, New York, but it gave no street address. There was a printed name of Hannah, just as my grandmother had once told my father.

How I wish that he could be here now to see his authentic birth certificate, this would have made him so happy to know that someone has finally taken an interest in something that he wondered about all his life. I hope my father is looking down at me and smiling.

My hopes of finding her are positively reinforced. In fact, I am more determined than ever to find her.

At that moment, for some unexplained reason, I remembered the strange feeling that came over my father when he was in that old church in County Mayo, Ireland. I thought there might be a connection there. I needed records from Ireland and Yorktown, New York. I proceed to the library to order them. Again, they tell me that it will take about two to three weeks to receive them. That didn't bother me, as I was use to waiting.

After about a week and a half, I receive a call telling me that some of the records I ordered had arrived. I quickly hang up the phone, grab the keys, and run to my truck. I spend the rest of the day reading the Irish census from 1860 to 1900. The census from 1900 had not come in yet. I find the name O'Connor in County Mayo. In Fact there are quite a few of them. But I can't find a Hannah O'Connor.

I make copies of everything I can find and take them home with me. I sit down in my father's favorite chair hoping that these old records and my penny will take me back in time.

Chapter Eleven

Sarah

As I enter into a state of deep concentrate the room begins to fade in and out.

#

I am no longer in my house. I'm in a time and place I've never been before. It takes me sometime to realize where I am. The scenery is breath-taking! There are beautiful green rolling hills with sheep grazing and stone walls everywhere. I look down at myself and I'm in different clothes again. Clothes from an even earlier time than before.

I'm clutching my penny in my hand. As I look closer, I see a Catholic Church. There appears to be a convent on the side and a small well landscaped cemetery. From photos I had seen, it looks like the same church in Ireland, that my mother and father were in when my father had that strange feeling come over him. The church looks much newer. It's made of stone, and in the front there is a tower that surmounts the rest of the building. At the top of the tower there are openings. I can see the bells that are silenced now. From the looks of my clothes, it appears to be in the middle to late 1800s.

As I walk towards the church, I'm side tracked. In the distance I can see a quaint little village. I feel compelled to walk in that direction. After going a short distance, I notice a group of people on the edge of town dressed in black and carrying a coffin. It's obvious that they are going to a cemetery. I hear the beautiful mystical sound of a lonely tin flute in the distance, as it echoes through the hills.

The cemetery is different than the one on the church grounds which seemed to be reserved for clergy. I follow the procession. There are three girls walking at the head of the procession holding hands with a woman. I assume that she is their mother. One of the girls appears to be maybe about fifteen or sixteen years old with red hair and fair complexion. The other two are a bit older. I watch them in the cemetery. People are crying and holding one another.

I hear the priest saying, "Charles O'Connor was a good hard working family man who always put his family first, his beloved wife Mary, his three daughters Irene, Elizabeth and Sarah. He always had food on the table. Charles was always one to remember a limerick. He once told me that when times are rough, remember to forget the things that make you sad, but never forget to remember the things that make you glad. Mary, Irene, Elizabeth and Sarah, he was referring to you when he said, to remember the things that make you glad. Now let us pray the Our Father."

The priest blesses the coffin and sprinkles it with holy water as it is being lowered in to the ground. "And may the soul of Charles O'Connor join all the souls of the faithful departed. May he rest in peace, amen."

I follow as everyone walks back towards the village. I feel that this has to be the family that I am in search of. Mary, Irene, Elizabeth and Sarah live on the out skirts of town. It's a pretty stone house with a thatched roof that stands alone. I watch some of the towns people that knew Charles take food to the family. They talk of the old days, telling the girls that they would not remember the potato famine because it was before their time and that their father was a boy then.

They tell how his family struggled to stay alive along with the rest of them. They talk of happy times, and tell the family that Charles is in a better place now.

The O'Connor family has always been farmers raising geese for market, and cows for milk. Piled in front of the house, are bogs that are used for fuel to heat the house in winter. It's not an easy life, it's hard work and the girls try to keep up the best they can.

They attend mass regularly with their mother and the girls attend a small school close by. Sarah seems to take more of an interest in the church than her sisters. She watches the nuns at the near-by convent working in the garden. This is the same church and convent where I was before I was drawn away by the funeral procession. She wonders what other things the sisters do in their daily lives. Her mother tells her that in this particular order they pray a lot and help the poor by making clothes. She tells her that to be in the convent, it takes a special person, because they make huge sacrifices. Sarah tells her mother that she wants to help people and especially the poor. Her mother is deeply religious but worries that Sarah may be hasty in her thinking. She is young and there are other things in life that she has not experienced yet, like having a family of her own someday. She tells Sarah that she should wait for just a little while. Sarah continues to observe the sisters when she can, and the more she watches, the more she becomes interested about their lifestyle.

On the convent grounds there is a lovely garden with a statue of Mary protected by a large stone wall. I walk inside the church; it looks just like the pictures my parents had taken. There are large life like statues of saints in every corner. Walking around, I notice the distinct smell of incense. There are a few older sisters praying in the pews and an older priest. He is the same priest that knew Sarah's father. He walks into the confessional. Sarah walks into the church and sits alone praying. A few of the sisters know her from seeing her all the time. When it's her turn, she enters the confessional and when she comes out, she lights a candle and prays. She returns to her pew. When the priest is through, he comes out of the confessional and speaks to one of the older sisters. I take it that she is the mother superior.

She turns and looks at Sarah and walks over to her. She tells Sarah to come with her, and they walk to the sacristy.

The mother superior tells Sarah, "Sit down my child. Father tells me that you are interested in joining the convent."

"Yes I am Sister."

The priest enters the room and sits with them.

Sarah tells them, "I have already spoken to my mother about this."

The mother superior gives her a stern look and says, "That's fine my child, but what are the reasons that made you decide that you want to join our order?"

"I want to serve God and help the poor, Sister."

The priest and sister accept her answer and approve her decision to enter the convent.

They tell her to return home to tell her family, because once she commits herself to the order, she will be in the convent most of the time working and having little contact with the outside world. Only a few of the older sisters are allowed to leave once a week to deliver clothes to the poor.

Her hair is cut by one of the other sisters, and I watch as she takes her vows of poverty, chastity and obedience with a few other girls her age. There is the melodic sound of a nuns choir in the loft behind the church singing in Latin. This holy ceremony must be closed to outsiders, because only nuns are in the pews watching.

Although her mother and sisters don't live far from the church, she only sees them when they come to mass, and all but a few of the sisters are forbidden to speak to outsiders. Sarah has given her life to Jesus and her church. She along with the others work hard making clothes for the poor, praying, and gardening.

About a year goes by and Sarah has adapted very well to the rigid routine. There are two elderly resident priests in the church. One of them, the priest that officiated over Sarah's father's funeral became ill and died. Not long after, a new, younger priest arrives. His name is Father Francis. He is introduced to everyone. He then takes on his priestly duties of hearing confessions and conducting mass.

There is something about him that I don't trust, I can't put my finger on it, but he seems as though he is hiding something. He watches the sisters and begins to give Sarah more attention. I notice, He seems overly friendly towards her and he looks at her in a way a man, not a priest, would look at a woman. When he does this, at first Sarah shyly looks away, and tries to ignore it. This continues for a few weeks.

Sarah begins getting use to it and accepts it, thinking maybe this is the way he is. One morning after mass, Sarah is walking towards the garden, Father Francis catches up with her.

As they are walking he tells her, "Ever since I arrived here I have been attracted to you..."

Sarah interrupts, "Father do you realize what you are saying? You can't mean this! You are a priest and I am a nun this is a sin, the worst sin!"

Father Francis says, "Please listen, I'm torn, I know it isn't right and I have taken my vow of celibacy but my human weakness is taking over. I know my spiritual side must win, but my feelings for you are too strong. Sarah I love you."

"Oh Father this isn't right!" she replies, as she continues walking.

Father Francis tells her, "Please meet me in the garden tonight at midnight so we can talk."

Sarah walks away without saying anything further. For the rest of the day, she thinks about what he had told her and she couldn't get this off of her mind.

Night came, and after everyone goes to sleep, Sarah walks to her window. The full moon is out. In the garden, she sees him sitting on a bench waiting. Suddenly she too falls prey to her human instincts. She quietly leaves her room and walks outside and before she reaches the spot where he is sitting, he turns and looks.

"Sarah, I'm so glad you came."

He walks to her and takes her hand. She knows what she is doing is wrong, but for some reason she can't hold her feelings back. They walk beyond the garden. He takes her into his arms and they kiss. This is a nun and a priest who succumb to their physical feelings and had forgotten their vows. I am shocked at what I am seeing and I want to yell at her to stop his advances, but she is young. No one has ever given her this kind of attention. Sarah is naive. She truly believes that Father Francis cares for her. This brief encounter turns into an affair. He tells her that he wants to take her away from the convent and be with her forever.

Her mother's concern for her was justifiable. She was too young when she made her decision to join the convent. I could tell that she had fallen in love with Father Francis, and he seemed to be genuine in his feelings towards her.

They continue to meet secretly for a few months, although not as much as they did in the beginning. No one ever suspects that anything is going on. During the day Sarah works her regular routine in the sewing room and garden. When she prays, I can see that she is troubled. She feels guilty and knows that she has sinned. In her daily prayers, she begins to ask God to forgive her for her weakness.

I begin to notice that Sarah is feeling sick at certain times of the day. This goes on for some time. Other symptoms occur, which leads Sarah to realize she is pregnant. I think to myself, I knew this was going to happen. She is overwhelmed with confusion and fear. She fears that someone will soon find out, and wonders what to do and how long she can conceal her condition. She immediately goes to Father Francis.

She is sure that he will help her.

"Francis," she said in a low tone of voice. "I must speak to you!"

"What's wrong Sarah?"

She takes him to the side and whispers, "I'm with child!"

He looks at her astonished and replies in a whisper, "What!"

Again she repeats, "I'm with child and I don't know what to do!"

He asks, "Does anyone know about this?"

"No, I don't dare tell anyone."

His face begins to turn red, he is worried. He walks to the window and looks out for a few seconds. With his back still facing Sarah, he asks, "Who is the father?"

I can't believe what I am hearing and neither can Sarah.

She walks towards the window, and before she reaches him, he turns to her and with a firm voice and cold look asking her again, "Who is the father, Sister Sarah?"

Again, I can't believe this. He isn't calling her Sarah anymore, now it's Sister Sarah, and he has the nerve to ask who the father is.

Sarah tells him, "Francis, how can you say these things, you know that you are the only one that I have ever been with. You said that you wanted to take me away from here and be with me forever. Now is our chance."

He doesn't answer. Instead in a defiant tone of voice, he tells her to leave the sacristy, and insists that this conversation never took place. Then he says, "If you try to tell anyone they will never believe you."

"But Francis you must help me, I have no one else!" Sarah said.

He looks at her and says, "There is nothing I can do for you."

With that he turns and leaves the room.

"Father don't leave me!" she cries. But her cries are in vain, she never saw this coming. She stands there alone. She now realizes that he didn't love her at all. Sarah saw a side of him that he hid so well from her.

I knew that there was something about him, when I first saw him looking at her. I didn't trust him from the beginning.

Sarah is devastated as she has no one to turn to. This pregnancy will cause her shame both in and out of the church. This will stay with her for as long as she lives.

Standing there watching the events unfold. I feel helpless knowing I can't help her.

She begins to pray a lot in church. Father Francis goes on with his regular duties. He acts as though nothing has happened and ignores her whenever possible. As months go by, it becomes more difficult for her to hide her pregnancy. Her emotions are out of control; she must confront him for her own sake. He vehemently denies ever having a relationship with her.

He tells her, "If what you are telling me is true and you are with child, then you have broken all of the sacred vows you took to join the convent. I must report this."

She runs out of the office only to see that some of the other sisters and the pastor of the church have heard everything. In a way Sarah is happy that they heard. Maybe they will see the truth.

The pastor then walks in to talk with Father Francis.

"What is going on?" he asked.

Father Francis tells him, "She has gotten pregnant by someone and she was afraid to tell anyone, so she came to me."

"We must do something about this," the pastor said.

Thinking for a few seconds, he looks at Father Francis and says, "There is only one thing we can do."

He summons the mother superior. By now she has heard what has happened. She goes to Sarah's room and confronts her.

Sarah tells her, "It's true, I'm going to have a baby and Father Francis is the father."

On hearing this, the mother superior becomes angry and slaps Sarah. She then gives her some neatly folded clothes. Sarah looks at them and recognizes them as the clothes she was wearing when she first arrived. She tells her to put them on, and when she is finished, meet her at the front door of the convent. Sarah changes and walks slowly towards the front doors. There waiting is the pastor and the mother superior. She takes Sarah's habit from her.

The pastor tells her, "You are a disgrace to yourself and to the church. You have destroyed what is sacred. You are to leave this place and never walk into another Catholic Church for as long as you live. In the eyes of the church you are dead."

He then tells the mother superior to burn Sarah's habit.

These words hurt the most. As she leaves the convent crying, she turns back to look one more time and notices a dark figure behind the window curtain on the fourth floor of the rectory. It is Father Francis staring at her. She can see the cold look on his face. She believed that he truly cared for her, but he only used her. She turns back around and walks away from the church.

With nowhere to go, she moves back in with her mother and sisters. Her mother accepts her, as her love for Sarah is unconditional. Sarah is lonely and confused. Everyone knows that she has been in the convent and it doesn't take long, for news to get around in the village, that she is with child. Village people stare and talk about her. She knows her life will never be the same. Her mother is a good woman and she defends Sarah, but people still talk.

Fortunately Sarah's mother had been saving money through the years. One day she tells Sarah, "I have been saving this money since your father was alive for an emergency. I know the suffering you have endured here. It might be best that you take this and leave Ireland."

"But mother this is your hard earned money," Sarah said.

Her mother explains, "Sarah this is family money, it's for who ever needs it. I would do the same for your sisters if they needed it."

Sarah says, "Oh mother, I hate leaving you..."

Her mother interrupts, "Sarah you must leave this place, life will never be the same here for you."

"Where will I go mother?" Sarah asked.

Her mother replies, "Sarah take you and your unborn child to America. You can start a new life there. You know they say America is rich with opportunity. Sarah if you stay here you will be scorned by everyone and your poor child will feel the effects of this. Think of your poor innocent child Sarah!"

"Oh mother I should have listened to you when you told me to wait to join the convent." Sarah said.

Her mother tells her, "Sarah what's done is done. God and I know that you have always been a good child, and God forgives."

"Mother I wish that I could do something for you."

Her mother simply replies, "Raise, and above all, protect your child. That's what you can do for me."

Sarah packs her belongings, says good-bye to her mother and sisters, and boards a ship bound for New York. I step on board with her. I notice it's full of Irish immigrants. The ship is overcrowded and the conditions are terrible. I had heard they nick named these ships coffin ships. Now I know why. Weeks later, we arrive in New York.

I can tell she is scared, but that doesn't stop her from doing what she knows she has to do.

Chapter Twelve

Hannah

We get off the ship in a place called Castle Garden located at the tip of Manhattan. Here she changes her money and gets information about where to live. This looks like a tough place and Sarah knows it isn't going to be easy.

Not too far from where she got off the boat, she hears of a neighborhood on the lower east side where there are a lot of Irish immigrants living. As she proceeds there, she notices how dirty and crowded the streets are. People seem poor and some are living in the streets. Her first day in the city isn't pleasant at all. Because it was nearly the end of the day when she arrived, she isn't able to find a place to live, so she spends her first night in America sleeping on a door step. She is very careful with her money, as she no longer has a trust in people. She ties her belongings that are in her bag to her arm so no one can steal them. Lucky the weather is warm or else she would not have made it through a winter's night.

The next day she begins her search for a place to live. There seems to be more Irish here than there was in Ireland, and everyone has an Irish brogue. There is a tenement building with a sign, "Rooms for rent." The landlord is there and he is putting someone's things in the street for not paying their rent on time. Sarah talks to him, and he insists on getting paid on time. He tells her, he will not tolerate late payment, not even one day.

Jobs available to Irish immigrants, seem to be jobs that no one else wants. A lot of men become laborers. While others learn skills and work as shoemakers, bricklayers, carpenters and ironworkers. A few get a little luckier by getting inside jobs. Some become business men, by opening local pubs. Times are rough, so Sarah needs to find a job before her money runs out. She needs to save the money her mother gave her. She knows that she needs to venture out to see what kind of jobs are out there. There has to be something she can do. On the edge of this Irish neighborhood, there is a factory that makes clothes. She does know how to sew. She applies and is hired on the spot. I see a calendar on the wall it's August 20th, 1878. She works long hours for little pay and there are bosses for every section. They walk around to make sure that everyone is keeping up. These bosses are not very nice to their employees. They are constantly down their backs, telling them to keep up.

This is a sweat shop and it is really getting on my nerves watching these people treating other people so bad. Sarah is very good at sewing, because of her experience at the convent. So it isn't hard for her to keep up. She comes to work everyday and says very little.

She does make one friend by the name of Kate at work, that lives in the same building as her.

Sarah's baby is due any day now. One night after work, as she is walking up the stairs to her room, Sarah goes into hard labor and screams for help. Kate her neighbor hears the commotion in the hallway, and looks out to see what is going on. She sees that Sarah needs immediate help. There is no time to get a mid-wife. She helps Sarah to her room.

Shortly there after a beautiful baby girl is born. It is September 5, 1878. She names her baby Hannah. I get a chill down my spine when I hear the name Hannah. I knew that someday this would be my father's birth mother.

Even after what happened to her in Ireland, Sarah holds no resentment towards the church. She always remembers where she is from.

She continues holding on to her Irish Catholic roots. That would always be a part of her. Deep in her heart she wants Hannah to be baptized Catholic. But remembering what the priest had told her, she did not want to step foot into a church, thinking it would be another sin, and she did not want anything bad to happen to Hannah. Knowing that her neighbor Kate is Catholic, she asks her if she would take Hannah to be baptized. She tells Kate that she is not a Catholic, but wants Hannah to be baptized Catholic. Kate happily agrees. Sarah weeps as she stands outside the church waiting, wishing she could watch her baby's christening.

Hannah is a pretty baby, with blue eyes and reddish hair. She is quiet baby, and only cries when she is hungry. It's a soft, very gentle cry. I can see that Sarah loves Hannah very much.

A few days pass and Kate comes over to visit. She tells Sarah that the boss at the factory told her to tell Sarah that she no longer has a job, and to not even bother coming back. Sarah said that she kind of expected this to happen. She still has more than enough money, at least for a month or two of rent and food, that her mother had given her. But she doesn't want to use it all up. So in a couple of weeks she begins looking for another job. With all that Sarah has been through, I notice with time, that she has become hardened and tough.

Sarah wants the best for little Hannah. She does not want her to grow up in this rough neighborhood. Again, she ventures out to look for work beyond her neighborhood and the clothes factory. She gets up early every morning with Hannah and walks to the trolley, which takes her to different parts of the city. It is difficult looking for work. No one wants to hire a woman carrying a small baby with her. Day after day she continues the same routine. Until one day her luck changes. As she is walking a man stops her and tells her he has recently opened a hardware store and that he is wanting someone to help out. He tells Sarah that he has a large family and that his wife had been helping him until she became too busy with their own children.

He tells her, "I have been noticing you looking for work in the neighborhood for the last week or so. Would you like to work for me? I can pay you two dollars a day. I know it's not a whole lot of money but the hours are good and I'm fair. I know you have a baby, she can come with you too."

Sarah tells him, "My name is Sarah O'Connor and this is my daughter Hannah."

He smiles and replies, "My name is Thomas O'Mally, It's very nice to meet you. Would you like to come in so I can show you around?"

"Yes I would," Sarah replied.

Thomas asks, "When would you like to start?"

"I can start right now if you can use me."

"It's a deal," said Thomas.

Time has passed. The year is 1886. Things seem to be much better.

Sarah has taught Hannah how to read. They no longer live in Irish town.

They have found a place closer to the hardware store and Sarah continues to save her money.

Sarah writes to her mother in Ireland.

> Dear mother,
>
> I think of you often and miss you. Hannah is eight years of age now, you would be so proud of her. She has learned to read and write from my home teaching. She is a wonderful daughter and I have been fortunate enough to work for a very nice man, who has allowed Hannah to come to work with me, since she was a baby. I have never told anyone of my past and I suspect that I will continue to keep this dark terrible event, a secret through my live. I would never want anyone to know, especially Hannah. You once told me above all to protect Hannah. I have been doing so. Mother, I would never have survived in the streets of New York if you hadn't given me support. I will never forget that. Oh mother, I wish that you could meet Hannah, she is very special. I hope that someday I will be able to repay you for what you have done for me and Hannah.
>
> Your loving daughter,
>
> Sarah.

A few days later, Sarah and Hannah are walking to work. They are about a block from the store, when Sarah slows down. She has a bad feeling before it even happens. She stands there for a few seconds. All of a sudden a shot goes off and a man runs out of the store. Sarah steps in front of Hannah to protect her as the man runs away. They run into the store, there is a strange silence. Thomas O'Mally's wife runs downstairs and screams, as she sees her husband laying on the floor next to an open cash register. Sarah yells for help, and both women crouch down beside Thomas, trying to comfort him. He tries to speak. He is more concerned about his family than himself. The children stand behind their mother as she cries. Within a few minutes the police arrive. Thomas is fighting for his life. He had been shot in the chest at close range. I can see the pain as he tries to breath. He looks at his wife and family as they weep. Barely able to speak, he tells his wife that he is sorry. A few minutes later he dies. The room is full of sorrow. There was only ten dollars in the cash register and it was gone.

The family tries to run the hardware store themselves, but they can no longer afford to keep Sarah. She is left to fend for herself again.

Hannah has turned ten years old now and Sarah ends up getting odd jobs here and there. She is strong willed and where ever she goes, Hannah goes with her. She is a good mother and loves Hannah very much.

It's hard for her to find a steady job. Maybe I'm wrong, but I get the feeling that people don't want to hire a woman with a child and no husband.

One day while looking for work, Sarah walks into a small grocery store. She tells Hannah to wait outside for her, which she rarely did.

She always keeps a close watch on Hannah and is very protective. As she is waiting to talk to someone, she glances out the store window and notices, that a gang of young hoodlums have approached Hannah and begin taunting her. Well, she comes out of the store swinging. I guess her Irish temper kicked in and the gang scattered.

Sarah has had enough and she decides it's time for her and Hannah to move away from the city. They gather what little belongings they have and head for the train station. They look at all the destinations on the wall. Not knowing where all these places are and what they are like, she chooses one and asks the ticket agent if this is a nice town.

He tells them all the towns outside the city are nice.

So she points and says, "We want to go there."

The agent replies, "That's Yorktown mam! You're just in time, the train leaves in ten minutes."

They pay the agent and board the train, as they hear the conductor holler, "Last call for Yorktown."

Sarah and Hannah are quiet as they look out the window. They begin to see a different world from the city. They stop at all these quaint little towns and villages. They watch as the people get on and off the train and they listen as the conductor calls out the names of the towns at every stop. The country side is beautiful and there are large estates everywhere. This all looks like something out of a story book. Sarah and Hannah are in awe. They never imagined anything existed like these mansions. How can people afford to live like this? They reach a town not too far from the estates they had just passed.

The conductor hollers, "Yorktown coming up!"

The train comes to a stop.

Again, the conductor hollers, "Yorktown, last call for Yorktown!"

He looks at Sarah and Hannah and says, "Ladies I believe this is your stop."

Sarah replies, "Yes thank you, it is."

They get off the train and look around. It's a pretty town.

Sarah looks at Hannah and says, "This is home Hannah. We are finally home."

"Oh mother I'm so glad that you are happy."

Sarah looks at Hannah and tells her, "Everything I do in life I do for you Hannah. You are my life."

They walk for a while and the people are friendly. Everyone seems to know one another as they nod when they pass by. The men tip their hats to the ladies. I notice that Sarah is not overly friendly towards the men, as she tries to ignore them and look the other way. I think, that she thinks, that they are being flirtatious. Without any trouble, they find a place to live about a block from the center of town.

Hannah is proud of her mother and wants to repay her for everything that she has done for her. Hannah expresses this to her mother, but Sarah only sighs and tells her that she loves her and she does not have to repay her. Hannah is a kind, caring and gentle girl.

Sarah has done a good job in raising her. Sarah continues to be very overprotective of

Hannah. She has never really let her out of her sight since the day she was born.

Sarah hears of a small factory on the edge of town that makes coats. It is a fairly new shop, owned by one person. She hears they are hiring. So she goes to inquire about it. This is nothing like the factory in the city where she worked before. That which seemed so many years ago. This is clean and the working conditions are very good.

People get two breaks a day, and a half an hour for lunch. It is owned by one man and there aren't bosses looking down your back every minute.

She applies and tells the owner, whose name is Theodore Smith that she is very experienced and that she will produce. I can tell that she is suspicious of every man she meets. She just doesn't trust them. She tells him that she is new to the area and has an eleven year old daughter, that is no trouble. She asks if it would be okay that she come along until school starts in a couple of months. He agrees, and Sarah starts the next morning.

Sarah and Hannah get up early every morning and when they get off at night, they cook supper and talk for a while. When it's nice they sit outside. It's a quiet place. All I can hear is the clunking of the horse's hoofs, the rattle of the buggies as they pass by, and a few children playing in the distance.

Sarah writes to her mother in Ireland.

> Dear mother,
>
> I know that I have not written you lately. Due to the circumstances, I have not been able to. Hannah and I moved away

> from the city. I feared that it was not a good place to raise my precious Hannah. The past years have not been the best, but we have settled in a small town that I think we can finally call home. I have a good job sewing in a coat factory. I am hoping that you can meet Hannah someday as she is my pride and joy. She is a kind and gentle girl. My life revolves around her. Now that we are settled, I promise to write to you more frequently.
>
> As always your loving daughter,
>
> Sarah.

Sarah never talks of her past to Hannah. She does talk about her mother in Ireland every now and then, but Hannah wonders about her father. Sarah never talks of Hannah's father and I suspect she never will. She just tells Hannah that her father died just after she was born. That's when she decided to come to America. She keeps the past to herself. Hannah is a sensible girl and is not one to probe in to other peoples business. She seems like the kind of girl who figures if someone wants to talk about something, then they will.

There is a family of eight living a couple of doors down from Sarah and Hannah. They seem to be a nice close knit family. They had seen Sarah and Hannah several times on their way home from work, but never had a chance to talk. One day after work, the mother comes by with an apple pie and introduces herself. She apologizes for not coming over sooner, but she knew that Sarah worked and didn't want to impose.

Sarah thanks her for her hospitality and introduces herself and Hannah.

The mother then said, that she had a couple of children that looked like they might be Hannah's age and invited Hannah to come over sometime. When she said those words, I could see Sarah's expression change. Sarah politely refuses, but thanks her for the offer. Hannah is beginning to notice that Sarah is becoming more protective. Although she never asks, I can see she begins to wonder why her mother does not allow her to play with the other children.

In time Sarah does allow Hannah to attend school. There is a two room schoolhouse in town. One is used for the younger children and the other room for the older children. There are a few children in each class. Because she can read and write, Hannah is placed with the older children. At school, Hannah keeps to herself. She does well with her studies. Because her mother purposely kept Hannah by her side all of her life, she really never had a chance to make friends. So it is very hard for her. She almost feels guilty when she talks to others. She feels that her mother is her only friend and she doesn't want to let her down.

It's been quite some time since Sarah has heard from her mother.

One day Sarah receives a letter from Ireland.

> Dear Sarah,
>
> I am writing this letter to inform you that mother passed away suddenly several weeks ago. She received your last letter telling her of your move and new job. She died shortly there

after. Sarah, she was always worried about you and hearing this news made her so happy. It was a small ceremony, as most of her friends have passed away since you left. We buried her next to father. We will place a flower there for you.

Your sister,
Irene.

Sarah is broken hearted as she loved her mother very much. I think she was saddened mostly by the fact of knowing that she would never meet Hannah.

Sarah continues to work in the clothes factory. About a year passes and Theodore, Sarah's boss calls Sarah to his office. Sarah doesn't know what is going on. She looks worried.

Theodore tells her, "Sarah come in and sit down. Sarah you told me the day I hired you, that you could produce. Well you were right, you have excelled in production. You are one of the best workers I have ever had. I would like to offer you a position as manager, that's if you want the job."

Sarah breathed a sigh of relief.

"Are you okay?" he asked.

Sarah replies, "Oh yes sir, I'm fine. I thought that you called me in here to tell me you didn't need me anymore."

"Oh no,no Sarah! I need help and I thought that you would be excellent for the job."

"Yes I would love the job," Sarah said.

She thanked him and he tells her to begin immediately.

Things are going very well for Sarah and Hannah. After school Hannah comes to the factory to help out. Theodore is very good to the both of them. He develops a fondness for Sarah, and Sarah is perceptive of this. She ignores it. She has never had another relationship with a man since the affair with the priest. She has never forgotten that day in Ireland. She would never trust another man. She was just not interested.

I knew how she felt and I didn't blame her. I was the only one that knew her secret.

The more she got to know Theodore, the more she trusted him.

After he saw that Sarah was not interested, he didn't bother her much, and she noticed this and respected him. She began to see him as he really was, a sincere man, different than the others. He had helped her so much without ever asking for anything in return.

As time passes Sarah accepts his attention. He is a fine gentleman and he treats Sarah like a lady, which she deserves. He is kind to Hannah and treats her like a daughter. He genuinely wants to take care of them. He asks Sarah to marry him. After thinking about it for a few days, she realizes, that she is in love with him, and believes he is in love with her.

I never thought that I would see the day that Sarah would ever trust another man enough to marry.

Within a few months they are married. She had never forgotten what the priest told her that fateful day when she left the convent.

She believed that it would be a sin to step into a church, and that her marriage would be doomed from the beginning. There is no choice, the Justice of the Peace would have to marry them. The ceremony is small, as only a few people are invited. Most are workers from the factory.

Sarah never forgot where she came from, and she never wanted her workers to suffer the same conditions that she experienced, when she was working in that sweat shop in New York City. Sarah's workers respected her. Sarah hoped that Hannah would have a better life. She did not want her to struggle like she did.

The business grows and Theodore becomes very prosperous. They move into a middle class neighborhood. The house is a two story granite home surrounded by tall oak and maple trees that hover over it, as though they are protecting the family inside.

A few years pass and Hannah has turned into a beautiful young woman. Sarah still protects her as she always has, especially from young men that show an interest. Sarah doesn't trust any of them.

Hannah has never understood this, but never questioned her mother. I was thinking that maybe some of Sarah's thinking may have rubbed off on Hannah. After all, Hannah is still very close to her mother, and regards her as her mentor. She always listens to what her mother tells her because, she always seemed to be right. It's like Hannah is still tied to her mother's apron strings, through no choice of her own.

Theodore continues to provide a good life for the family. Sarah no longer works; she doesn't have to. She is a comfortable housewife.

She belongs to the local ladies groups and her money problems are a thing of the past.

#

Without notice, the faces of Sarah and Hannah begin to blur. I know this feeling. I know what is happening. I struggle to stay, but the wind is too strong. It whirls me up and I'm flung back into my father's chair in my house. Clinched in my right hand is my Indian head penny. Again, the clothes I had on back then, have turned so old and raggedy, they are about to fall apart. I look down and see that the census records had ended too early. I wasn't sure, but it seemed as though I was close to finding out what happened to Hannah. I am so frustrated.

Chapter Thirteen

Between Heaven And Earth

I immediately call the library. By now they know me by name. They inform me that they have the city directories for Manhattan, and the 1905 to 1920 census for Manhattan and Yorktown.

I quickly change my clothes and rush out to the driveway, and jump in my truck. As I'm putting the keys into the ignition, I look at myself in the rearview mirror and notice wrinkles that hadn't been there before. I have circles under my eyes. It looks like I haven't slept in weeks. But I can't give up now. I am completely obsessed. I set my penny on the dashboard and head for town. After driving a few miles, I stop at a red signal light. As I wait for the light to turn green, I think about all that's happened to me, and all the places I have been. I think to myself, am I going nuts? Or am I actually seeing my family grow up. I slap myself in the face and look in the mirror. I still look worn out. And what about Hannah, is she my father's mother?

This has to be her. If so, what happened to her? The light turns green and the car in front of me enters the highway intersection. I follow at a slow pace, when all of a sudden, a pickup truck runs the red light and rams into my drivers side door. The momentum, pushes me sideways about twenty feet. Everything seems to be going in slow motion, as my truck flips over several times and comes to a rest upside down. With the engine still running, there is smoke, glass and metal everywhere.

Somehow I manage to crawl out of the passenger's side window. Unable to go far, I lay down in the street waiting for someone to help. I can just barely hear people's voices asking me if I'm all right. My vision is blurred and I can hear sirens in the distance. Finally, everything becomes clear and the pain I'm in is no longer there. I see a blue sky and in the distance, a figure standing by itself. Something is pulling me slowly in that direction. As I get closer, I see a familiar face.

It's my father! He is holding his arms out to me.

"Daddy where am I?" I asked.

He looks at me and in a quiet tone of voice he says, "Your between heaven and earth like I am, but it's not your time yet Tommy. I know how you have felt for many years. I just wanted to tell you, that when we are alive on earth, things happen that we don't quite understand. I knew that when you returned home from Vietnam you were different in many ways, but that experience has given you strength and vision, that a lot of others don't have. I know you feel bad that you left Madison, and me and your mother, but that was your destiny."

"Daddy, I feel that I let you and mommy down when I left. I don't know why I left or what I was looking for. I missed being around you for the last twenty years, doing things with you, like the others.

Spending all the holidays with you, helping you when you needed something done around the house, when you weren't able to do it yourself. Walking in the woods with you. All these events, I missed.

Daddy you never really got to see my family grow up. I'll never forgive myself for leaving Madison, the town where I grew up, and where my heart still remains."

"Tommy, I know what you have been thinking, that's why you were chosen to do this little job for me. This will be a healing for you. Now, you need to finish what you started, to help me get beyond this point. And when you are through, you need to go back and take care of your family, and visit your mother as much as you can. They need you."

"But we need you," I said.

"I was old and tired Tommy. It was my time, I don't feel any pain here. You can do more for me if you go back."

And with that, he fades away and the sounds of voices and faces of people are coming back to me. I am riding in the back of an EMS ambulance, with its sirens on and a nurse taking my blood pressure.

The nurse looks at me and says, "We almost lost you back there."

Then he continues to ask me questions like my name, age and where I lived. He does this for quite sometime. I guess to keep me from going into shock. Then something occurred to me, I laid my penny on the dashboard of my truck when I left home. I told the nurse that I lost something.

"Don't worry, the police will find whatever you lost."

I said, "I am worried, I had something on my dashboard that I have to have!"

The nurse doesn't answer.

The next day, I awake in the hospital. My wife and daughters are here, and the first thing that comes to my mind is my penny and wondering where my truck is. I ask them if they could find out where it has been towed and to try to find my penny. They do and return to say that my truck was damaged beyond repair. They said they looked everywhere, but they couldn't find anything. They said that part of my windshield was missing and because of all the damage, they weren't able to get into the truck.

I think to myself, "How stupid, I can't believe I put the penny on the dashboard and not in my pocket!"

After being in the hospital for a few days, I am finally released. I never told anyone that I had seen my father after the accident. I kept it to myself. But seeing him made me more obsessed. I knew without me, he was unable to get out of what he called, between heaven and earth. I wanted so much to help him. I went to look for the penny myself; I even went to the accident site. It had rained really hard since the accident. I knew that it had probably washed away. I scoured the roadside, then went to the junkyard and looked through my truck, what was left of it.

Looking at the mangled wreck I say to myself, "I should have been killed that day."

After hours of searching, I finally give up. I went back the next day and several times after, but found nothing.

Weeks go by. In deep depression, I don't want to leave the house.

I study the records over and over. I sit in my father's chair and think about where I was and where I needed to be, hoping to go back in time, but nothing happens. I lose interest in everything. Thinking, I can't go on like this forever, I think about going to a coin collector to see if they have a similar penny. After making several stops around town, I finally find one. Excited, I rush home and sit in my father's chair with the same old ragged clothes I had on when I came back.

I close my eyes and think of Sarah, Hannah, and Theodore and what things looked like when I left there. I say their names over and over and over again. Instead of going back to Yorktown, I fall asleep. When I awaken, I'm still in my father's chair. The penny is of no use, because it's not my father's penny. I sit and wait for hours, but nothing happens.

My heart feels so empty and I feel so alone. I came so close to finding out what happened to my father's mother. At a point of exhaustion, I decide to go to bed. I can't think about this anymore.

About a week goes by and I decide to fly up to Madison to visit my mother. She isn't getting out of the house much now. She does manage to go the grocery store a couple of times a week and never misses mass. She seems so quiet and it feels so lonely in the house, as only memories remain. As I look around, many of the same things are in the house that were there when they built the house. My father's chair still remains. And downstairs in the basement are all of his old overcoats. His old traps lay in another corner. His work shoes still sit in front of the old couch, where he would change after coming in from working outside. There are tools from the early 1900s that my father used, when he worked with his father. Upstairs in my old bedroom, most of the things still remain the way they were, when I was in school.

I decide to take a trip to the foundling in New York City. I had to continue my search for my father's family. After talking to the sisters for sometime, I realize I am getting nowhere. I think maybe the library will have something. I did find some interesting history about the foundling. I find a quiet spot in a corner and begin to read. There were several orphanages in New York City during the late 1800s and early 1900s. The Children's Aid Society and the Foundling Home, were two of the largest in the city. While here, I begin looking through some old census that have lists of the names of children that were in these orphanages during my father's time. It was my unlucky fortune that he wasn't listed because he wasn't born until October, 1905. The census was taken in June of that year.

I went back to stay with my mother for a couple of weeks. I took her to church and helped do some things around the house. The neat yard that my father kept so nice, had become overgrown and it takes me a few days to get everything back in shape, but it would never look as good as when my father did it.

We visit the cemetery often, I plant daffodils and bring a folding chair, so my mother can sit and watch. It makes her happy to know that someone cares. Keeping your loved-one's grave clean is still a priority. Then we get in the car and drive through the cemetery. It seems as though mommy knows everyone here. We stop at the plot where her mother and father are, and she sits silently looking at their stone. It's been nearly sixty years since her mother Concetta has passed away.

After arriving home, I look at my father's empty chair and imagined him sitting there telling stories. I remember while on my venture into the past, what I had seen in Madison when my father was a boy. Those were such good times.

My mother senses that not being able to finish what I started is bothering me.

"Why don't you take my car and go up to Yorktown. Maybe you can find some information there or find the old house they lived in, and ask around, maybe someone will remember something. It won't hurt to try," she said.

I decide to take her advice. The following day, I drive up to Yorktown. As I'm driving, I'm thinking, I can't be going just to be going. I need to accomplish something! I find a library and begin looking through old phone books and city directories. Fortunately, they have both resources from the 1920s to the present. I decide to rent a room near-by and stay for a couple of days. The following morning, as I am drinking a cup of coffee at a diner, I'm looking out the window.

Something looks familiar. As I look closer, I feel like I know what I am looking at. I get up and quickly pay for my coffee and walk outside.

Right then, I knew where I was. I had actually been here. It is the house that Sarah and Hannah lived in, when I last saw them. It was the same pretty house with the towering oak and maple trees that hovered over it, as though they were on guard. I stand in front and watch for a while. I finally get enough nerve to knock on the front door.

A young woman answers, "Can I help you?" she asks.

I stuttered, thinking that I would see someone else answer, like maybe Hannah.

I said, "I'm... sorry to bother you mam, but I had a relative that once lived here. I lost contact with her through the years.

Maybe you knew her. Her name was Hannah O'Connor, she lived here for many years."

The woman replies, "No, my husband and I have been living here for five years and I don't recall anyone by that name."

I thank her and apologize for intruding and walk back towards the street.

Then I heard the woman's voice, "Sir," she said.

I turned and looked.

She walked through the front door with something in her hand and said, "We found this old photo in the attic when we first moved in. It was so attractive, that we knew we had to keep it. We figured that it must have been a previous owner."

She turned the photo so I could see it. I was overwhelmed with emotion.

I said, "Yes, that's her, that's Hannah, she was my grandmother.

She was very young in this photo."

The photo was beautiful. She looked radiant and looked so much like my father it was amazing. I couldn't take my eyes off of her.

She was just as I remembered her, with that kind and gentle look.

The woman said, "Why don't you take it? It really belongs to you, she is your grandmother, we really don't have any use for it."

"Oh thank you," I said. "But it was in your house, I feel odd taking it from you."

"We just kept it because it was in the house. You need to take it, it's yours," she said.

I thanked her and walked back to the street. Everything looked so familiar. I drove to the edge of town. The house where Sarah lived when she first arrived, is still here. It hasn't changed much. Instead of the clunking sound of the horse and buggy, there are cars. I wanted so much to go back and see Sarah and Hannah.

I drive back to Madison and stay at my mother's house for another couple of days. When I leave, I tell her that I will be back soon. On my flight back to Texas, hundreds of thoughts are going through my mind. I had to figure out a way to get back in time. I needed my father's Indian head penny.

Another month goes by. The more time that passes, it seems the less of a chance that I will ever go back. One day, the phone rings.

When I answer it, I hear a woman's voice. She says that she had witnessed my vehicle accident. She explained, "I was driving the car in front of you. If that had been me that day, I would have been killed because I was in a small car. Well anyway, the reason that I'm calling you is I was wondering if you had lost something that day?"

I said, "Yes a lot of things fell out of my truck that day, but the most important thing was an old Indian head penny that my father once gave me. I carried it everywhere."

She said, "As soon as I saw the accident, I ran towards you along with everyone else, to see if I could do anything to help. After they took you in the ambulance and I was done talking to the police, I was walking back to my car when I saw this unique penny on the ground, quite a ways from where your truck was. I picked it up and thought it was from someone's collection of old coins. For the last month or so, I have been thinking about its owner. Something told me it might be yours and I thought I should return it to you."

Excited I said, "I can't believe this, I am so glad you called, that penny means so much to me! You just can't imagine."

We arranged to meet. Driving over there I thought, my father must have had a hand in this. The woman did say, something told her that it might be mine and that she should return it. It was just too coincidental. When I got my penny back, I put it in my pocket and not on the dashboard. Like an obsession, I kept feeling my pocket to see if it was still there. I couldn't believe I got it back.

The ride home seems to be taking forever. When I get to the house, I can't seem to move fast enough. I have to calm down. I dress in those raggedy old clothes again and gather all of my records.

Finally, gathering my composure, I sit in my father's chair. I feel so relieved and hopeful. I sit for a few minutes to gather my thoughts and try to remember, where I was and what I was doing when I last saw Sarah and Hannah. I feel I have to do everything right, because this was my last hope of getting back there. If this doesn't work then nothing will. I even go so far as to take the pictures off the wall that remind me of the present. I get the photo of Hannah that the lady in Yorktown found in her attic. I hang it in front of me and I stare at her. Her eyes seem to be making contact with me and following me around the room. With my penny clutched tightly in my hand, I slowly reach for all the records on the table next to my chair. Then I close my eyes and block out everything from the present.

#

In a minute I begin spinning down the spiral hole. Everything that I had seen was passing me by. I can see where I am headed in the distance. It is back to Sarah, Hannah and Theodore's house.

I look down at myself and I'm wearing new clothes. I hear voices inside. I walk through a side door and into the kitchen. I see a calendar on the wall, it's 1902. Hannah is twenty four now. I look over my shoulder and see her sitting at the kitchen table with her mother.

They are talking to a gentleman in a suit. He appears to be a lawyer and they are signing some papers. From their discussions, I realize that Sarah's husband Theodore, recently died from a massive heart attack. In his will he stated that in the event something happened to him, he did not want Sarah to have to worry about keeping the business going. He stated that the business be sold, and all the money go to both Sarah and Hannah. From what I gathered, this had already taken place. He hands them a check for a very large sum of money, and tells them that they will never have to worry about money for the rest of their lives. I can tell that this is bittersweet news. Sarah loved Theodore more than she would ever admit.

Sarah and Hannah stay in the same house that Theodore left to them. Sarah continues to keep her few lady friends in town, and Hannah stays mostly to herself. Although they could, they choose not to live a lavish life style. They remember what it was like to be poor and how difficult it was to get money.

Chapter Fourteen

The Affair

One day while walking home from the neighborhood store with a bag of groceries, Hannah rounds a corner. Out of nowhere, a young fellow runs right into her, causing her to drop her groceries all over the sidewalk and the street. Shyly, she begins to pick them up and the stranger helps, while apologizing. He is a tall handsome fellow with dark wavy hair and a soft spoken voice. By his mannerisms he seems to be as shy as Hannah. They never look directly into each others eyes. Again he apologizes saying, "I'm so sorry! It was my fault, I didn't see you coming around that corner. I should have been watching where I was going, I was in a hurry to get back to work. Your bag is torn let me go get you another."

Finally making eye contact Hannah replies, "No I can manage, I don't live far from here."

He says, "Please let me help you, I feel bad! You can't carry those by yourself."

Hannah agrees. They don't say very much while they are walking because Hannah's house is so close. They get to the front door and she walks quickly, so her mother doesn't see them. Without a good-bye, Hannah opens the front door glancing back at him. He just stands there watching her. I notice a slight smile in her blue eyes as she closes the door behind her. She never tells her mother of the incident, as she knows what her mother thinks of most men.

A few days pass and Hannah is on her way to the store again. She passes the livery stable and she sees him, the same handsome man walking out with a horse. At first thought, she thinks of turning around and walking the other way to avoid him, but changes her mind and continues on. He notices her and walks over to her.

He says, "I'm sorry I didn't properly introduce myself the other day, but I felt so bad about what happened, that it completely slipped my mind." Extending his hand he says, "My name is Patrick Coyne, what's yours?"

Returning the hand shake, Hannah replies, "My name is Hannah..."

Stuttering as though she is trying not to reveal her last name. Finally saying, "O'Connor."

Patrick says, "Ah That's a nice Irish name, are you from Ireland"?

"No," replies Hannah. "I'm from here. Do you live in the area? I hadn't seen you before we bumped into one another that day."

Patrick says, "No I'm not from here in Yorktown, I'm from Ohio originally. My family came from Ireland during the potato famine and settled there. That's where I was born. My father died when I was twelve."

I can see that Hannah is enjoying the small talk and Patrick's gentleman like attitude. But she is beginning to look a little concerned that maybe her mother might come by and see her, and she knows that her mother would not approve of him.

So she said, "I have someone waiting for me, I really must go."

Patrick says, "I should get back to work also. Can we talk again sometime?"

Hannah replies, "Maybe sometime, we'll see."

I can see that Hannah is fond of Patrick. She stops to see him every so often and they talk, but only for a short time. Patrick notices this, but he never questions her about it.

As time goes on, Hannah makes her regular trips to the store and always stops to talk with Patrick. Patrick wants to spend more time with Hannah, but she tells him that it would not be a good idea. She explains that her mother is very protective and doesn't trust very many people. Sarah begins to notice that Hannah is spending more time away from home, especially on her so called trips to the store. She realizes that for some reason Hannah loves going to the store. Hannah cannot resist Patrick's charm anymore. They begin spending more time together walking at a near-by park. They are so comfortable with each other, that they don't have to say anything. I watch as they walk hand in hand. Their love grows from friendship to passion. They begin an affair. Patrick wonders why They have to meet secretly. He thinks that it would be better if Hannah's mother knew the truth. But she doesn't want to ruin the love that they have, so she doesn't tell her mother.

Hannah tells him, "Patrick, you don't know my mother. She is a good person and a loving mother, but she has a very difficult time trusting people, especially men. I don't know why, but she has been like this ever since I was a little girl. It's better that we meet like this."

I think to myself, Hannah is much too old to be so controlled by her mother. But on the other hand it's been going on for so long that it's like a way of life, and Hannah has always respected her mother for what she has done for her.

I think Sarah suspects something, but I also think that maybe she thinks that this will pass, but it doesn't. To find out for sure, Sarah follows Hannah one day and she watches as they meet in front of the livery stable. Her suspicions are confirmed. That's all she needed to see. Sarah sees herself in Hannah. She suddenly feels the memories of what happened to her as though it were yesterday. To her, this man that has an attraction to Hannah, reminds her of Father Francis back in Ireland. Sarah still sees Hannah as her young naive innocent child. She turns quietly and goes back home. When Hannah returns, Sarah is quiet at first.

Hannah notices and asks, "Mother is something bothering you? You seem awfully quiet."

Sarah replies, "Hannah I've tried to raise you the best I could by bringing us out of poverty and teaching you right from wrong. Let me get to the point. I know that you have been seeing that young man from the livery stable and before it goes any further it needs to stop."

Hannah replies, "Yes mother, I have been seeing him. He is nice to me and I like being with him. No one has ever treated me like he does."

"Hannah, he is just a livery man with no future. He seems as though he may be a drifter moving from town to town. Where is he from?

I know he is not from this area. What is his background?"

"He is from Ohio mother, and he is Irish."

Sarah then asks, "Why is he here Hannah? You don't know what you are up against if you stay with him. Hannah, I don't want you to see him anymore!"

"But mother," Hannah said. "I can't imagine not seeing him anymore."

"You have to do this Hannah. It's for your own good."

Hannah knew that this was going to happen sooner or later. She leaves the room and goes to her bedroom.

I can't believe how much influence Sarah has on her daughter. I think maybe it would have been better, if Sarah had told Hannah the truth about what happened to her when she was a young girl. Then Hannah would understand why her mother is the way she is. But I know that Sarah was too ashamed to tell anyone of her dark secret.

Hannah doesn't go out much. Patrick continues waiting for her, but she never shows up. He doesn't know what's going on, so he decides to go to her house. He believes that Sarah must have found out, and forbids Hannah to see him again. If this is so, then he needed to talk to Sarah. She needs to understand how he feels about Hannah.

Sarah answers the front door.

"Hello, my name is Patrick Coyne. I was wondering if I might be able to speak with Hannah?"

Sarah abruptly replies, "Hannah is not available to see anyone right now."

Patrick asks, "Is she not feeling well?"

"Yes, that's right she's not feeling well," Sarah rudely replied.

"Is there anything I can do to help?"

Sarah answers, "No we don't need help from anyone! I'm very busy right now."

She closes the front door and Patrick is left there standing alone. He turns around and heads back to the stable.

A couple of days pass and Patrick decides to go back to speak with Sarah again.

She answers the door and doesn't say anything.

"I'm sorry to bother you again, but I was wondering if Hannah might be feeling well enough that I might be able to see her?"

Sarah replies, "I don't think that it would be a good idea that you come here anymore, Hannah is much too busy."

In a soft spoken voice Patrick politely tells Sarah, "Please don't make me leave without seeing Hannah. I know you want the best for her, but I love her."

Sarah only hears what she wants to hear and when Patrick speaks, her mind wanders. Her mind flashes back to Father Francis and she remembers how difficult it was for her and Hannah.

Then she hears Patrick's voice again. "Please just give me a chance to..."

Sarah quickly interrupts, "You are a stranger to me and my daughter! You are not from this area. How do you think you can take care of Hannah on the money you make as a livery man, who drifts around from job to job, not knowing where you will land next! We have been poor, and I won't allow Hannah to live like that again. Let me tell you something, if you think that you are going to come around here, telling me that you care for my daughter hoping to move into a lavish life style, you've got another thing coming and you need to look elsewhere!

Now you need to leave. I don't want you knocking at my door anymore, and I don't want you bothering me or my daughter again."

Hannah hears almost everything from the kitchen. She is very hurt by what she heard. Her mother always knew best, but she is still confused as to why Sarah is so distrustful towards people especially men.

"Oh mother, I wished that you hadn't talked to Patrick in the way that you did. He is a kind and gentle person. Did you notice that he never even raised his voice or showed any disrespect towards you when you were telling him all of those terrible things? Mother, he doesn't have a mean bone in his body!"

As I stand there, I watch and listen, I feel sorry for all three of them. Patrick walks back to the stable and continues to work, but he is very sad.

Sarah tells Hannah, "Someday you will understand. As time goes by you will forget him. Hannah you are a beautiful young woman and I don't want you to fall prey for just anyone. He will soon forget you and find someone else of his own caliber."

Hannah and Patrick are able to secretly see one another a few more times. They dream of running away together, but Hannah could never leave her mother. They wish that she would change her mind and accept Patrick, but that seems unlikely. Patrick cannot take this secrecy any longer.

He tells her, "Hannah, meeting you like this has been very difficult. We are on pins and needles constantly wondering if someone will see us together. I want so much to be with you all of the time.

I'm not sleeping at night and when I'm working I think of you constantly. Hannah, I do love you more than anything and I want to be with you always and forever. But I don't think that will ever happen.

So I must tell you that I will be leaving in the morning. Please know that I will never forget you. No matter where I go or what I do, I will always hear your sweet gentle voice, and see your kind beautiful smile."

I watch as Hannah listens in silence. Tears are rolling down her cheeks.

Crying, Hannah says, "Please don't go Patrick. I love you so much. Maybe in time my mother will change her mind."

Patrick replies, "Hannah, I want to marry you, but I know that your mother will never allow that to happen and I know how close you are to her. I don't want to interfere with that. She brought you through what she said, were very hard times. Maybe she's right, maybe I am just a drifter going from job to job. Maybe I'm no good for you. She did a good job in raising you Hannah. I don't blame her for being so proud and protective of you. You were fine before you met me and you will be fine when I'm gone. Who ever your mother approves for you, he will be the luckiest man on this earth."

He wipes the tears from her face and they kiss. "Good-bye Hannah."

The next day, Hannah arrives at the train station as the train is leaving. She sees him sitting by the window in the next to the last car. His eyes well up with tears as he looks at her. Hannah watches the train until she can no longer see it. I can see the emptiness and devastation she is feeling in her face.

It's the summer of 1905, and a month has passed since Patrick has been gone. Hannah walks to the store and stops at the livery stable in hopes that Patrick might be there again, but he never is.

Not long after, she begins to feel ill. Believing that it might be the stress of not seeing him, she ignores it. But when it continues, her mother summons the family doctor. He goes to Hannah's room to examine her. After being there for a few minutes, he walks out to the hallway where Sarah is waiting.

"Sarah," he said, "Hannah is pregnant."

Sarah looks at him with surprise and says, "What? This can't be!

Are you sure? Please tell me it isn't so!"

"Sarah, you know I've been a doctor for many years, I know when someone is pregnant. I am absolutely positive that Hannah is pregnant,"

Sarah looks as though she is going to faint. Offering his assistance, he tells her to sit. "Are you going to be okay Sarah?"

"I'll be okay, I just need to sit here for a few minutes. Doctor when is the baby due?"

"Maybe late September or early October."

She stares at the wall in front of her as though she is in another world. Just what she was trying to prevent from happening, happened anyway.

Sarah realizes that Hannah is repeating her own mistakes. The thought of this is unbearable. She doesn't want Hannah to feel the same shame and embarrassment that she felt all those years ago.

As I watched Sarah, I thought of her as a victim and I couldn't really blame her for thinking the way she did. She wasn't a bad person for trying to protect her daughter. What happened to her back then at the convent, changed her life and twisted her way of thinking.

Scared, Sarah has to prevent anyone from finding out. As time goes on, Hannah's pregnancy starts to show. She doesn't go out much. In August Sarah approaches Hannah.

She tells her, "Hannah, you know that we are not going to be able to keep this child. We would be a disgrace if word got out that you had a baby and no one knew who the father was."

"But mother we know who the father is!"

"Even if it is him Hannah, he is gone and you are not married everyone knows this."

"Mother, I know it's him he is the only man I have ever loved and been with. What if I find him, then we can get married."

"Hannah, you don't even know where he is, he is a drifter, moving from place to place!"

Hannah angrily replies, "Mother you drove him off! He wanted to stay, but you would not allow him to see me anymore. Mother he told me he loved me and he wanted me to run away with him, but I wouldn't do it because I didn't want to leave you alone mother. He told me that he could not meet in secrecy anymore. He said that he didn't think that you would ever accept him. So he decided to leave."

"Hannah, look how he left you pregnant and unwed."

"Mother you raised me without a husband!"

Sarah says, "Hannah this will be a child born out of wedlock and people will know this. We live in a small town and the child will suffer as it grows up. I don't want to be the talk of the town. We have always had a good standing in this community. Hannah we are going to give this baby a good home by letting someone adopt the child. I seem to recall that there was a very nice orphanage in New York City that places children in good homes. We will leave here on the first of the month and find a place to live for a short time until the baby is born.

Then we will take the baby and go to the orphanage. When we leave here, people will wonder where we are going. We will tell them, that we are going on a trip, to visit some relatives up state."

Desperately, Hannah begs, "Mother I'm asking you to reconsider, I know Patrick is coming back. I will tell him, then we can marry."

I watched as Hannah spoke. It's as though Hannah is talking to a wall. Sarah didn't hear a word she said.

Sarah keeps talking, "And while we are in the city, we will keep a very low profile and keep to ourselves."

Sarah doesn't listen, her mind is made up.

On September 5, 1905, Sarah and Hannah board a train for New York City.

Chapter Fifteen

The Birth And The Loss

They find a place to live on 125th Street. Although she hasn't been back in years, Sarah still knows her way around the city. It's a nice neighborhood, with a line of pretty brown stone houses on both sides of a cobblestone street. The building that they choose to stay in is a long white brick three story boarding house. It definitely stands out from the rest of the brown buildings. Sarah knows that no one would know them in this neighborhood, and it is far enough away from home, that no one will ever know that Hannah was pregnant.

Hannah stays in her room most of the time. She really has no desire to go anywhere. She looks out the window at the children playing. I know that she is depressed. Luckily a mother and her young daughter move in next door. Hannah and the young girl, who appears to be about fourteen, become friends. Her name is Addie McDonnell and when she is not in school, she visits Hannah.

Just after midnight on Thursday October 12th, 1905, Hannah goes into labor, Addie and her mother hear the commotion and come next door to help. It goes on for hours and by daylight a baby is born. It's a boy, Hannah is filled with love and pride. He is a beautiful baby and just as Hannah did when she was a baby, he only cries when he is hungry. And when he does cry, it's a soft gentle cry. Hannah loves him and gets as close to him as she can. I watch as she holds him. There are times it seems as though she has forgotten that he will no longer be hers.

Addie comes over everyday after school to visit the new baby. She and Hannah talk and Addie holds him. They still need to name the baby and because of her religious background, Sarah is familiar with the saints and their feast days. She explains to Hannah that naming him after a saint will protect him. The saint that they choose is St. Edwin his feast day is October 12th. Edwin was a Catholic from England, and the king of Northumbria. He reigned for many years. He was a man of wisdom who chose Catholicism because deep in his heart he felt that this was the faith he firmly believed in. Because he remained firm in what he believed, Edwin was slain in a battle against pagans on October 12, 663. Many churches were built in his honor in England.

Through all that happened to Sarah in the past, deep in her heart she remained a Catholic and firm in what she believed. Edwin was surely the appropriate name for Hannah's baby.

Sarah demands that he be baptized. Again, Sarah still feels that she should not go into the church, so she makes the excuse that she is not Catholic. Because Hannah was not well enough to go, Addie and her mother decide to take the baby themselves.

On Friday October 20th, 1905, Addie and her mother take baby Edwin to the church and knocked on the door of the rectory.

The priest answers and they tell him, "Father, we found this baby on our doorstep with this note."

The note that Sarah had devised said, Please baptize my baby for I am unable to keep him. I have named him Edwin because he was born on October 12, Saint Edwin's day. In naming him after a saint, I am hoping that this will take care of him and protect him from the evil's of this world. The note is signed, A distressed unwed mother.

To baptize the baby, he will need a sponsor. Addie quickly volunteers. The priest smiles, and baptizes Edwin. The certificate reads, Parents unknown, sponsor Addie McDonnell.

Addie and her mother take Edwin back to Hannah. They thank Addie for caring. Poor Addie never knew much about Hannah and Sarah. They told her and her mother that they were from Long Island. Sarah didn't want anyone to trace them back to Yorktown. She did not want anyone to know that Edwin ever existed. People could never find out that Hannah was pregnant.

One day while visiting, Addie asks Hannah, "Does Edwin have a daddy?"

In a soft tone of voice Hannah replies, "Yes Addie, Edwin has a wonderful dad."

Addie tells Hannah, "We used to live in a nice place, but my daddy died and we moved here. Did Edwin's daddy die too?"

"No," Hannah replied. "He just went away for a while."

Hannah begs her mother to keep Edwin. "Please mother, I love Edwin!"

She tells her mother that she can stay in the city and work until Patrick comes back, then they can marry.

Sarah explains, "Hannah, we are not staying in this city any longer than we have to. I am not leaving you here alone. How do you expect to work when you have a baby with you all of the time. No one will hire you. You will be in the streets like I was with you. I swore that I would never let that happen again. This city is tough Hannah.

You haven't been any further than this room. You don't know what it's like beyond here. How do you know what Patrick will do? He may never come back, and we are not going back home with a baby. Hannah, I told you that this day would come and we planned this a long time ago. There is no turning back. We've come to far. I promise you that Edwin will get a good home."

In the early morning hours of Friday November 10th, 1905, Hannah and Sarah gather their things together. They wait for Addie to go off to school. They wrap Edwin in a blanket and silently walk down the hallway to the stairs that takes them to the street. It's a cold, foggy, drizzly morning. Without looking back, they walk quickly away from Edwin's birth place, turn a corner, and get on a trolley, which takes them about three blocks from the foundling. Hannah weeps as she holds Edwin close to her heart. Hannah has taken good care of Edwin in the short time that she has been with him. She has grown attached to him and loves him dearly. This is one of the saddest days of her life.

Hannah cries and whispers in Edwin's ear, "I am so sorry Edwin. I love you so much, I wish that you could understand what I am saying to you. I will never forget you for as long as I live. I hope that someday, we find each other. Please don't forget me Edwin, and when you are old enough to understand, I hope you won't hold this against me.

Please know that in this world, people don't accept unwed mothers with children. I loved your father very much. He does not know about you, he went away before he found out about you. I know that if he were here, he would feel the same way as I do. My mother promised me that you will be placed in a good home with a loving family."

I wished that my father could be here to hear those words, as they echoed in my ears. It is so sad to watch Hannah carry Edwin for the last time.

As we walk through the fog, which had thickened considerably since we left the boarding house, I hear a near by church bell ring.

Then through the fog I see the foundling home. Both in tears, Hannah and Sarah enter the building. Sarah does not want to go inside because she knows that nuns run the home, but she also knows that she has to be supportive of Hannah. The inside was as I remembered it when Vincenzo and Antonetta came to pick Edwin up. They walk down the long hallway. I could see that even now Sarah, as strong as she is, has become weak. When they are about halfway down the hall, they are greeted by a sister. As they walk, Hannah holds little Edwin closer.

When they reach the front desk, they are led into a room that I hadn't seen before. It's called the receiving room. This is the room where all of the new babies are left. I noticed that it was separate from the rooms where the parents that were interested in adopting would come.

I'm supposing that they didn't want the adoptive parents and the distraught birth parents to see one another. The receiving room also has an exit of its own that leads to the side of the building.

Hannah cries as she tells the sister, "I am unwed and I can no longer care for my baby. I..."

No longer able to speak Sarah tells the sister, "We don't know where the father is. He left some time ago and has not returned."

The sister looks at Hannah and says, "I understand my child, he is in excellent hands with us. Have you named him?"

Hannah, still overwhelmed doesn't answer.

Sarah says, "Yes Sister we have, his name is Edwin. We named him after Saint Edwin, hoping that he will be protected through life."

The sister responds, "Ah yes, that's a good name. I'm aware of this saint. He was a man of wisdom and stayed firm in his belief's.

Only those who practice the Catholic religion very closely would know about these not so well known saints from England. You must be from a strong religious background."

Sarah replies, "Yes Sister, I am."

Then the sister looks at Hannah and goes on to say, "I know that this is a very difficult time for you, but if this gives you any consolation, I listened to what your mother has said, and by you having the courage to come in here today, we will make a note of all of this.

We will make absolutely sure that your baby Edwin is placed with a good family. Some of the mothers that leave their children with us don't go to the trouble of coming in with their babies like you and your mother did. Some just leave them at our doorstep and go away. I must tell you that you are very brave today, and God will bless you and your baby Edwin. Some of our parents are referred to us by their local church. I will make certain that Edwin is one of those children. I must tell you that in a few moments, we will have you sign a surrender, which will give us the same power which you possess as a parent. Once you sign the surrender, Edwin will be in our care for a period of his life. You may stay with him for just a little while, but it may be better if you limit your time with him. Please believe me, the longer you stay with him the harder it will be for you."

As she signs the surrender, Hannah holds Edwin close to her and sobs. Hannah kisses Edwin. She then hands Edwin over to the sister.

Edwin cries, Hannah cannot bear to hear him cry, as she knows that he only cries when he is hungry. Sarah puts her arm around Hannah and they slowly walk away.

Hannah turns and whispers, "Good-bye Edwin, I'll love you forever."

They fade away into the fog.

They return home to Yorktown and get on with their lives, but Hannah cannot get Edwin off of her mind.

A year goes by, and Hannah tells her mother that she is going to New York City to see if Edwin is still there. Her mother reminds her that it will be very traumatic for her if she sees him.

Hannah explains, "Mother I just want to see him."

Sarah replies, "What good is it going to do Hannah? If he is there it will hurt you to see him, and if he is not there you will wonder where he is. You need to let him get on with his life."

"Mother I don't care, I feel I need to do this."

Against her mother's wishes Hannah takes a train into the city by herself and she rents a room not too far from the foundling. The next day she gets up early and waits across the street. She watches, as the sisters take the children for their walks to near-by Central Park. As she follows them to the park, she notices one little boy with blond hair and blue eyes, sitting on a sisters lap. He appears to be about one year old, the age that Edwin would be. Hannah lovingly watches from behind a tree. Her motherly instinct tells her that it is Edwin. He is a beautiful baby. She sees him giggle and smile at the sister. She wants so much to hold him.

She walks over and sits next to the sister, and in her soft voice says, "Oh what a beautiful baby."

She can't take her eyes off of him.

The sister tells Hannah, "He is one of our best behaved babies.

Everyone at the foundling loves him."

I believed that, because through out his life, my father was loved by all.

Hannah asks, "Would it be okay if I hold him?"

Hannah holds Edwin once more.

"What's his name?" Hannah asked.

"Edwin," the sister said.

I could see the love in her eyes. She whispers, "I love you."

The sister never suspects that Hannah is the mother, or maybe she does, but she doesn't show it.

Holding him that day was not enough, so Hannah decides to stay in the city for another couple of weeks. Everyday she waits for the sisters to take the children for their walks and watches inconspicuously from a distance. She enjoys watching her baby play.

It's November, and the weather is beginning to turn too cold for the sisters to take the children out for their walks. Hannah waits, but she no longer sees Edwin.

She returns to Yorktown. She tries to forget and keeps busy.

Although she doesn't have to work, because thanks to Theodore, her and her mother are financially secure, she takes a job as a nanny. But even though she is busy in her new job, she never forgets Edwin. By now she has accepted the fact that Patrick wasn't coming back. She never had another relationship. She had only one love, Patrick.

Chapter Sixteen

The Tragedy

The seasons came and went. Hannah never went back to the foundling. It was too painful for her to see her baby, knowing that she would never be able to have him.

The year is 1909. Four years have passed since Hannah last saw Edwin or Patrick. She is enjoying the fragrance of the wild roses as she walks to the store. It's a beautiful morning. As she gets closer to the store, she glances over towards the livery stable. She sees a man working on a sign up over the roof. Suddenly she stops and looks closer. She looks as though she doesn't believe what she is seeing. The man working on the sign, looks like Patrick. She moves closer and she realizes that it is him. She had always kept just a glimmer of hope that he might someday return. She dreamed of this moment.

"Patrick!" she calls.

He turns, looks, and starts down the ladder. He walks to Hannah and they stare deep into each others eyes.

"Hannah, I've missed you so!"

They embrace and there is a moment of silence.

"Oh Patrick, I knew you would come back."

Patrick looks at Hannah and says, "Hannah not a day has gone by that I haven't thought about you. I knew that your mother would never accept me but I had to come back so I could see you again, even if it was just to see you walking to the store. It would be better than not seeing you at all."

"Oh Patrick, I'm so glad you returned. So many things have happened since you've been gone."

She looks at him and in her soft tone of voice she says, "Patrick, we have a son!"

Patrick sits down when he hears this and Hannah sits next to him.

He looks at her and in a loving voice asks, "Where is he? Can I see him?"

With tears in her eyes, she begins to tell Patrick, "After you left, only about a month after, I began to get signs that I was pregnant. Oh Patrick, if I could have only gotten you to stay a while longer! Patrick, we don't have him anymore." Hannah cries as she tells him, "My mother would not allow me to keep him. She didn't want anyone in town to know that I was an unwed mother, so we put him up for adoption."

"Hannah I'm so sorry, but I could not live in this town knowing that I could never have you. Hannah, I love you and I always have."

"And I love you too," Hannah said.

"What did you name him?" Patrick asks.

"I named him Edwin. He was born on October 12th, and my mother thought that it would be fitting that we name him after Saint Edwin an English saint, whose feast day is on Edwin's birthday."

"Edwin, that's a nice name. Is he in an orphanage near-by? Maybe we can go there and try to get him back," Patrick said.

Hannah replies, "My mother did not want anyone to know about him so we took him to a very large foundling home in New York City. We rented a room about ten blocks away. In the early morning hours of October 12th, 1905, he was born in that room. We kept him for a month.

Oh Patrick, it was so hard for me to give him up! I went there about a year later to see if I could find him. I stayed for a while and I would watch the sisters, as they took the children for their walks. I saw him Patrick! I knew it was him the moment I saw him. I asked the sister his name, and she told me Edwin. Patrick I held him! He had such a beautiful smile and sparkling blue eyes."

"He has your eyes and smile Hannah," Patrick said.

Crying, Hannah tells Patrick, "It was too heart breaking for me to stay any longer knowing that I had given him up. I feel so guilty Patrick!"

Patrick hugs Hannah and says, "I wish that we could get him back and marry. I want to go to this foundling home and see if he is still there, maybe I can get him back."

Overjoyed, Hannah returns home and tells her mother that Patrick has returned, and he wants to try and get Edwin back. Sarah is skeptical of Patrick's intentions. She certainly does not trust him. he got her daughter pregnant and left town. She is also doubtful that the child would still be there.

I could tell that Sarah was not very happy with all this news.

She tells Hannah, "Even if he were there Hannah, what do you think you are going to do, just walk in there and tell them, yes Sister, that man who used me and got me pregnant, decided to come back after almost five years and I would like my child back? Hannah, it just doesn't work like that. You signed a surrender that day saying that you could no longer care for your baby. That paper you signed gave the foundling complete and total custody of the baby to do what they see fit. And that was to find him a good home. You are no longer his parent, the foundling is, and they decide what is in the best interest for the baby. Oh Hannah you don't know the world around you. Put this behind you and get on with your life."

Hannah replies, "What life mother, I don't have much of a life! I don't know the world around me, because you would never let me go far enough to see how the world looked. Please mother, at least let him try."

Sarah tells Hannah, "I can't stop him from going there, but I do know he will be wasting his time. He will not accomplish anything, rules are rules."

That next morning Patrick boards a train for the city. He then rides a trolley that takes him about three blocks from the foundling.

This is the same path that Hannah, Sarah and Edwin had taken a few years before. He walks to the main desk where a sister is sitting. He explains who he is. The sister listens and appears to be unimpressed with his story.

Coldly, she responds, "That child is no longer here, and I am not at liberty to give out any more information. We have laws that we must follow. Once a child is adopted and removed from here, his or her records are sealed. I am sorry that I can't be of more help."

Frustrated, Patrick leaves and heads back to Yorktown. Hannah had told him that her mother said he was wasting his time. She was right.

He continued to work at the stable. Hannah and him remain friends, but their relationship would never be like before. They would see one another wave and talk. I think they still love one another, but he knew that he could never have Hannah. He works long hours and keeps to himself. The only thing that really keeps him going is knowing that the only woman he ever loved, lives in the same town. Sarah never does warm up to him, but she didn't shun him altogether. I think she saw some good in him when he went to the foundling to try to find out about Edwin. She never said too much, but I could tell what she was thinking.

The town is growing and the stable is full. One night in early fall, there is a fire in the stable. There are horses stuck in their stalls in the back of the stable. The screaming horses and the smell of smoke awakens Patrick. He runs to the stable and tries to save the horses. The smoke is heavy, the fire is out of control, and he can barely see. He continues to enter the burning building. The scene is chaotic as Patrick frantically tries to save the horses. It's the middle of the night and I'm wondering when someone will call for more help. Exhausted, he enters the stable to get the last couple of horses out. They don't see him, and in the smoke they panic, and run through the front doors of the stable. Patrick is knocked to the ground and trampled. Barely able to get up, he crawls through the front doors, where an onlooker sees him, and pulls him away from the burning building to the side of the road.

Someone asks, "Is there anyone else in there?"

The onlooker says, "I think he was the only one, someone call a doctor! He sure must care a lot about those horses! He wouldn't let up until they were all out. I hope he's okay."

But he's not okay. I watch, as he lays there gasping for breath.

The onlooker is bending down trying to comfort Patrick, but he is becoming weaker.

The doctor arrives and tends to him, but it's too late.

Patrick whispers in the doctors ear, "Please tell Hannah I love her, tell her I will wait for.. her.."

Seconds later, Patrick dies.

The doctor knew Hannah and Sarah and that same night, he goes to their house. Knocking on the door he wakes them both. Sarah answers the door first, with Hannah standing in the background.

"Sarah, is Hannah here?" he asks.

"Yes, is there something wrong?" Sarah asks.

"There's been an accident Sarah."

Hannah hears this and walks up behind her mother, "What is it? What's happened?"

The doctor tells them, "There was a fire at the stables..."

Hannah interrupts with her voice trembling, she asks, "Where is Patrick?"

The doctor replies, "I tried to do what I could, but he was to badly injured."

He then looks Hannah straight in the eye and tells her, "Hannah, in Patrick's last dying breath, he told me that he wanted you to know that he loved you. He told me to tell you that he will wait for you."

Sarah turns to Hannah and tries to hold her up as she begins to faint. The doctor tells Sarah to take her to her room, so she can lay down. He gives her something to calm her and Sarah stays by Hannah's side. Sarah sits and stares at the wall until finally falling asleep herself. When morning comes, Hannah awakes to find Sarah by her side.

Sarah is sick with guilt. She puts her hand on Hannah's forehead and tells her that she loves her. Hannah tells her mother that she wants to go to the stable where Patrick was last.

As they approach the stable which is still smoldering, Hannah kneels, puts her head to the ground and weeps. Sarah cries for Hannah.

She is at a loss for words. She tries to comfort her, but no words or actions will help Hannah now. For she has lost the love of her life.

The owner of the stable is near-by and notices Hannah and her mother. He comes to comfort them.

He tells Hannah, "Patrick was a unique man, who loved you very much. He often spoke of you. Even though I never met you, I've seen you many times and I feel like I know you. I noticed in the last month or so, that Patrick seemed very lonely. I never really asked him what was bothering him, I suppose I should have, but he was a very private man and I didn't want to meddle. He was a good man, he saved the horses, but he didn't save himself. Please, if there is anything I can do..."

"You are so kind sir, thank you," Sarah said.

At the funeral, Hannah sees him laying in the coffin. She tells him that she loves him and she always will. Because he didn't know very many people in town, Hannah, Sarah and the stable owner are the only ones present. Sarah puts her arm around Hannah's shoulder to comfort her. Sarah feels that she is to blame for their separation. Her guilt is overwhelming.

Whispering in Hannah's ear she says, "Oh Hannah, I am truly sorry. I know now that he loved you very much. I know that I was overprotective. I was being selfish. I should have trusted your judgment, please forgive me."

Hannah doesn't respond, she just stands there, looking at Patrick holding on to his hand and silently crying.

The next day Patrick is taken to a small near-by cemetery. Sarah had purchased a family plot there when Theodore passed away. It is a small service. Sarah paid for all the funeral expense.

I watch as Hannah visits the cemetery everyday. They purchase a stone with an inscription that reads,

+

Patrick Coyne

Born 1875 Died 1911

My Dearest Patrick, You Faltered By The Wayside And The Angels Took You Home.

She spends hours working around the plot planting flowers and keeping everything clean. She sits in front of the stone, day dreams of them together and every now and then, talks to Patrick as though he were still here.

Months pass and Hannah is so lonely. She keeps to herself and stays in the house most of the time. She only goes out to visit the cemetery, then comes back home. She has isolated herself from the outside world. Her mother knows that she is depressed and it's not healthy. Sarah knows that she must break this cycle. Sarah tells Hannah that she wants to take her into New York City.

She says, "We can stay in a nice hotel and take a trip to the foundling, maybe we can find something out about Edwin. I don't want to get your hopes up but maybe, they can at least tell us if he was put into a good home. I think it will help you to get away for a while."

Although Sarah feels doubtful that they will obtain any information, she doesn't tell Hannah this.

I can see that Sarah is feeling guilty about all that has happened. Somehow she wants to make it up to Hannah. She wants Hannah to forgive her. Although Hannah never actually blamed her mother for the past, I know what Sarah is thinking. If it wasn't for her stubborn way of thinking, none of this would have ever happened. If she would have accepted Patrick, both Edwin and Patrick might still be here.

Protecting Hannah as much as she did was a mistake.

Hannah agrees to make the trip with her mother. They find a nice hotel not far from the foundling. It's a cold day in early March.

Although it's a different time of year, it reminds me of that day in 1905, when they left Edwin. Hannah feels as though it was yesterday.

Standing outside the foundling, she closes her eyes and remembers holding Edwin. She flashes back for a moment to the happiness she felt when Edwin was near her.

The foundling has grown in size, but the main building looks the same. Sadly, there are more children running around than there was six years before.

The sister at the front desk looks very familiar to me. I thought for a moment, then I remembered, she was Sister Vincent, the same sister that placed Edwin with Vincenzo and Antonetta. Sarah and Hannah tell the sister who they are, and the month and year they left Edwin.

They tell her the whole story about Patrick. The sister listens. Then she gets up from her desk and tells them that she will return shortly.

I follow her to a back room. I can see a large vault where hundreds of records are shelved. Skimming through the records, she glances up once in a while to look at Hannah and her mother, as they patiently wait.

The sister can tell that the women are fairly wealthy. But she could also tell that they hadn't always been like this. There was a humility emanating from them. She seems as though she really wants to help them.

Walking out of the vault she says, "Edwin was taken and placed with foster parents a few years ago. Unfortunately, I am not able to reveal his whereabouts, but I will tell you, I remember that he was talking when he left here. He was a quiet child and unusually good compared to some of the other children. All of the sisters missed him when he left. I see in the notes that before he left here, we were to make it a point that he be placed with a good family. If this makes you feel any better, he is healthy and in a very good home with a very nice couple that desperately wanted a child. We do have a nurse that visits the home to check on him periodically. This is all that I can tell you."

They thanked the sister. They knew what little information they did receive from her, was probably not supposed to be revealed, but she was kind enough to do it anyway.

Hannah asks her mother if they could go up to 125th Street to the boarding house where Edwin was born. She agrees and they board a trolley. Sarah is really trying desperately to show Hannah that she is sorry, and by making an effort to try to find Edwin, might help Hannah feel better.

As they pull up to the front of the building, nothing has changed. They walk in and climb the stairway to the hallway that leads them to their old room. They knock on the door, there is no answer and the door is locked. They walk next door to where Addie lived. An old woman answers. Sarah tells the woman that they are looking for a girl and her mother that once lived here. The woman tells them that she doesn't know them. A neighbor in the hallway overhears their conversation and tells them that she remembered them, but they moved out when the landlord raised the rent, and she didn't know where they went. Unable to find out anything more, they decided to go back home.

Hannah continues her routine of visiting the cemetery. Her mother and her begin to travel more. Every place Hannah goes, she imagines Edwin as a young boy. And when she sees boys playing, she thinks of Edwin and wishes that one of them would be him, and imagines him running up to her with a big smile and hugging her.

Chapter Seventeen

The Truth About Sarah

The years pass and it's 1920. Sarah is sixty years old. She is sitting in her rocking chair. I can sense that something is bothering her as she sits looking out her window, Hannah walks into the room.

Sarah says, "You know Hannah, I've been thinking a lot about this lately. There is a place that I would like you to see. I'd like to take you to where I was born in Ireland. I've never told you much about when I was a young girl growing up. I'd like for you to see your roots Hannah."

I knew that this had been bothering Sarah for quite sometime. She was getting older and thinking of the past more often. She never told anyone about what happened to her in Ireland. She kept this secret from Hannah for all these years. Maybe she's finally deciding it's time to tell Hannah the truth.

They purchase two first class tickets and board a ship bound for County Mayo Ireland. This trip is much different than when she left Ireland so many years ago. This is a cruise ship, nothing like the coffin ships that she and so many others came over on.

Hannah always knew that her mother was born in Ireland, but never much more than that. She is excited to finally visit the place where her mother was born and raised. Sarah had lost all contact with her older sisters since her mother died. She didn't even know if anyone was still alive.

When they arrive, they hire a horse and buggy to take them to her village. As they ride Sarah begins to remember the past. Nothing has changed. The stone houses with their thatched roofs, the beautiful green rolling hills surrounded with old stone walls, the villages and farms. This is the Ireland that she remembered as a child. Sarah never thought that she would see this place again. The sounds and smells take her back, and in the distance, she sees a house. It's the house that she was born in, the house where she said good-bye to her mother in, so many years before. She tells the driver to stop and wait. She tells Hannah that she wants to walk the rest of the way up the old dirt road to the house. The house is old and rundown with ivy growing through the broken windows. As she reaches the front door, she sees a lonely Irish orchid. Hannah picks it for her.

Sarah smells the flower and says, "My mother loved these orchids, she planted them in this spot."

She puts the flower gently in her pocket and says, "This was our home Hannah. My mother and father worked so hard. My father died when I was very young Hannah, he was a good man."

She takes Hannah by the hand, "This is where my sisters and I slept."

They walk back outside to where the buggy is waiting. She looks one last time as they drive away. She asks the driver to take them to the church next to the convent which can be seen in the distance. As they near the church, again, she asks the driver to stop so they can walk. As they get closer, memories flood back into her head. She tells Hannah that she walked this same road many years ago. As they walk through the big iron gates, Sarah pauses for a moment.

"Are you okay mother?" Hannah asks.

Sarah replies, "Yes Hannah, I'm fine I'm just remembering what someone once told me, when I was here last."

As they enter the grounds, they walk to a near-by bench and sit.

They sit in silence for a few moments.

"It's so beautiful here mother," Hannah says.

Sarah says, "Hannah something happened here many years ago, that I never told you or anyone else about. What I am about to tell you is shocking, but you must know."

Again, she flashes back as she calmly begins to tell her story.

"Hannah, I came here quite often as a young girl, I was deeply religious. Not long after my father passed away, I told my mother that I wanted to join the convent. My mother thought that I should wait, she said that I was too young, and that I should take more time to think about it. There was nothing else for me at the time, so I went against my mother's wishes and joined anyway. Yes Hannah, I was a nun and this secret has haunted me for many years. I had been here for awhile, and I performed all of my duties along with the other sisters. Then one day, a new priest arrived. His name was Father Francis. He became friendly with everyone, but he was overly friendly with me. I tried to ignore it at first. Oh Hannah, I was so young and naive! I had never been outside the village, and I suppose I liked the attention. He was a handsome man and he seemed kind and sincere. I trusted him, but one day his friendship went too far Hannah, and I gave in to him. We had started a secret love affair right here on these grounds.

Father Francis told me that he loved me and I believed him. We met for several months, then one day I found out that I was pregnant. I tried to hide it for as long as I could, but as time went on I knew that I was going to have to tell someone. I went to him Hannah, the man that told me he loved me. When I told him, he denied everything and told me that I had gotten pregnant by someone else. He told me that if I told anyone that he had gotten me pregnant, they would never believe me. Then he told me to leave his office and that he must report this incident. By now the pastor and some of the sisters had overheard him telling me to leave his office, but that's all they heard. When I left, the pastor went to question him about what was going on. He told the pastor that I had gotten pregnant by someone and that I came to him for help. Hannah, he denied everything. I knew that no one would believe me if I told them that a priest had gotten me pregnant, especially him. Oh Hannah, I felt so all alone."

"You should have told someone else mother," Hannah said.

Sarah replies, "It wouldn't have mattered Hannah. I was the one that was in the wrong, I was the one that was pregnant, no matter who the father would have been. It was bad enough to have a baby out of wedlock, but a nun having a baby? I felt like the lowest thing on this earth, I was a disgrace to the church. So that day, the mother superior came to my room. She handed me the clothes that I had on the day that I joined the convent. She told me to put them on and to meet her at the front doors. I did what she told me, and there she was, waiting with the pastor. It was then that they banished me from the church forever. The pastor told me never to set foot into another Catholic Church for as long as I lived. I felt like a curse had been placed on me that day Hannah, and that if I ever went into another Catholic Church, something bad would happen. When I handed the mother superior my nun's habit, I heard the pastor telling her to burn them. I'll never forget as I left that day, Father Francis looking out that window from behind a curtain." Sarah points to the window and tells Hannah, "It was that window right up there."

Hannah listens in silence.

Sarah continues, "I went home to my mother. I was the talk of the town. I couldn't go anywhere without someone staring or talking about me behind my back, and it was hard on my mother and sisters. My mother finally said, I think you should leave this place, for your own good and the good of your unborn child. She gave me some of her savings and told me to start a new life in America. So that's what I did Hannah, and you were born not too long after I reached New York. Hannah, since the day that I left this place I had a distrust in men. Theodore was one of the few that I found sincere, and it took me a very long time to realize that he was a good man, who genuinely cared about us. I know now that Patrick truly loved you. I just wish that I would have seen it before that tragic night, when his life ended. Hannah, I feel it was my fault for what happened that night, and if it wasn't for me you would still have Edwin. All I ever wanted to do was protect you Hannah, from doing the same thing that I did. Maybe I was cursed by that priest back then! But then I think a lot of good did come out of all this, because I have you Hannah. You are the kindest, sweetest daughter a mother could have. After what I put you through, I wouldn't blame you for not forgiving me.

Hannah you don't have a bad bone in your body. I wished that we could have gotten Edwin back so you would have had a little piece of your life back. I know that I have caused you to lose many years of your life, and I hope that you will forgive me."

Hannah says, "Mother I have always respected you. I was a little girl, but I remember how hard it was for you bringing me up all alone for all those years, with no one to help you. I always suspected that something made you the way you were. I'm glad you told me these things today."

They get up from the bench and walk together into the church.

Sarah hesitates momentarily as she walks through the front doors, as though she thinks something bad is going to happen. They sit in the last pew in silence. There are a few young sisters in the church preparing the altar for mass. Hannah and her mother get up and walk outside. On the side of the church is a small cemetery where some of the church clergy are buried.

Sarah stops when she sees one of the stones marked, Father Francis O'Toole Born 1850, Died 1885.

Sarah looks at Hannah with a tear in her eye and says, "That's your father Hannah."

There is a care taker close by, He's a jolly but scruffy kind of a fellow, that seems as though he may have had one too many drinks at the local pub.

Sarah asks, "Do you know anything about the priests that are buried here?"

She knows that stories in these little villages linger on for years.

With a strong Irish brogue the fellow looks at her and asks, "Which one do you want to know about?"

Sarah points and says, "That one."

"Ah yes that one," he said. "They found him laying on the ground just below that fourth floor window up there. They said he fell but a person would have to be pretty drunk to fall out of a window, don't you think? If you ask me, I think he jumped. The story goes that he had something going with a local girl, no one knows for sure. If it's true, I guess he couldn't live with himself anymore. Anyway, you know how those Irish tales are. Pardon me for asking ladies, but you look familiar, are you from the area?"

Sarah Replies, "No we're not from Ireland, we're from America.

Can you tell me what ever happened to that local girl?"

He looks down for a minute rubbing his chin then answers, "No one knows, one day she just disappeared. See that cemetery down there?

That's where her family is buried."

Then he walks off mumbling to himself.

Hannah and her mother walk back to the buggy. Sarah directs the driver to take them to the cemetery where her father is buried. As they ride, she remembers the lonely sound of that tin flute, that she heard the day they buried her father. They walk slowly looking at all the graves. Then she sees her father's stone, and next to her father is her mother. She died in 1892, and next to her mother are both of her sisters. One died in 1910 and the other in 1915. She stands there for a few minutes contemplating. Then she reaches into her pocket and gently pulls out the Irish orchid that she found earlier by the front door of her old house. She lays it on her mother's grave.

"This is your family Hannah, I wish that you could have met my mother," Sarah said.

They stay in Ireland for a few more days touring the country side. Hannah loves nature and appreciates the beauty of this magical isle. But Sarah also knows that this is not home anymore.

They return home and the years go by. They both keep to themselves not going out much. In August of 1930, Sarah dies in her sleep. Hannah came in to check on her, and knew immediately that she was gone. She was seventy years old. It's a small service with just a few people, as most of Sarah's friends are gone.

Hannah occasionally takes the train ride into New York City to the foundling. She gets a room at a near-by hotel and every morning she gets up early and sits across the street. She never goes in, she just sits and waits. She would stay for a week or two then go back home. She continued to do this well into the 1940s. She knows by now he must have a family of his own. But she never gives up hope.

I thought of the times that my father had gone to see if he could find her. They were both doing the same thing nearly at the same time, missing one another by a matter of months. They were so close to seeing one another but it never happened. I guess it wasn't meant to be.

Hannah finally stops going in 1946. It has become to difficult for her to travel. The city had changed so much. It seemed as though she knew it was too late. Even if she did find him, what would she say now, so many years later. She stays in her house rarely going out. She has her house keeper do her shopping for her.

As I look at Hannah, my grandmother I think to myself, she bares a striking resemblance to my father in looks, actions and her kind hearted ways. She gave him so many fine qualities. Oh how I wish they could have met.

On October 14th, 1949, two days after my father's birthday, Hannah's house keeper finds her slouched over in her rocking chair next to her window. She was seventy-one years old. She had never found what she was looking for. She had no other family. She is buried at the family plot next to Patrick, her mother and Theodore. By now the inheritance that Theodore had left them, was just about exhausted. What little was left was given to the foundling.

#

Everything starts to fade as it did before. I wake up in the present day. I'm happy that I had live through all of those events but at the same time I feel lonely. I had grown attached to everyone and now they were all gone.

I purchase a ticket and fly up to New York. I want to see Hannah's burial plot. I rent a car and make my way to the cemetery, I know exactly where she is buried. I had been here before but in a different time. Her stone is pretty, but I can tell that no one ever came here to visit. I'm sure that no one has been here since 1949.

Above her name is a baby with angel wings and the inscription reads,

When This You See Remember Me
And Think Of Me Not Unkind.
Although Your Face I Seldom See
Your Always On My Mind.

+

Hannah O'Connor

Thomas Sapio

Born September 5, 1878
Died October 14, 1949

A chill ran through my body when I read the inscription. On one of their visits to our house, when my children were growing up, my father said he awoke from a dream that he had of his mother and wrote down a poem. It was the same poem that was on his mothers stone. The strange thing is, he never knew his mother or where she was buried. He really didn't know what it meant or where it came from. He said, he just remembered it in the dream. He signed it and gave it to my daughters. He told me to frame it and hang it somewhere, and that's what I did. When I saw it on Hannah's stone in the cemetery, I knew, that even after she died she was trying to communicate with my father.

I decided to drive into the city to the boarding house on 125th Street, where my father was born. Everything has changed so much. There is an iron gate blocking the front entryway and all of the windows are boarded up. There is graffiti all over the walls. Instead of horses and buggies in the street, there is the sound of loud rap music coming from a near-by car. This is a rough neighborhood. I get out to look around.

I'm able to get in through a window in an alley on the side of the building. Again, I know exactly where I am going. I walk up the stairs and down the long hallway to the room where my father was born. There is no door and no furniture. The room is empty, except for me and the echo of my foot steps on the old wooden floors. It feels eerie walking around. The floors are creaking and the wind is blowing through the hallway making a howling sound.

The sounds outside in the street fade from my mind. I sit on the floor in the corner of the room. I can hear a baby's soft cry, and Hannah's gentle voice talking to him. It's as though the spirits are still in the building. I feel like my task is coming to an end here. As I leave, I turn to look one more time. Although my family had always known that my father wondered about his mother, and how he would say, I wish I knew her. No one else could ever feel the way I am feeling right now, I had seen it all.

I leave the city and return to Madison to stay with my mother. On September 12th, the day of my father's death, my mother has the 8:00 a.m. mass in remembrance of him, like she had done for the past ten years.

After church, we drive to the cemetery. I help my mother from the car and she watches quietly as I clean around the stone, something that I've always done since my father passed away. I know how much this means to my mother. We then go back to the house and sit in our favorite room talking. I told her everything that had happened to me and she listened intently. Although she didn't say much while I was talking, she seemed to know what was going on. After a while she dozes off. I get up and peer out the window at the old homestead. I think about everything I had seen. No one would ever believe me but it didn't matter, My father knew where I had been, and that's all that counted.

Turning away from the window, I looked over to his chair. He is sitting there.

He smiles and says, "Thank you Tommy, you did a good job."

My mother hears his voice and wakes up. She looks at the chair that she had seen him sit in for so many years. I thought she would be shocked, but it was like she was expecting him.

He looks at the both of us and says, "I will see you again someday. I'm so proud of you Tommy, you have helped me so much. I feel so good now Anne, but I miss you."

A tear rolls down her cheek as she listens.

"We all miss you daddy, I just wish that I could have spent more time with you."

He softly replies, "Tommy you have spent time with me, you were with me all of my life, you helped me find what I was looking for."

He walks to the window, hugs my mother and says, "I'll wait for you Anne."

He turns to me and says, "Take care of your mother."

"I will," I said.

Then a bright light appears over the front yard and gradually moves over the old homestead. He passes through the window and walks towards the light. He turns to look at us one last time. My mother and I have tears in our eyes.

He turns and walks to the top of the light, where Vincenzo, Antonetta, Concetta and Giuseppe are waiting. Then all of a sudden from beyond the light I see his old best friend Bocce running towards him, wagging his tail. He jumps into my father's arms and licks him. He walks a little further, and I see Hannah, Patrick and Sarah. They put their arms around one another. They finally found what they were looking for.

Their images fade away into the distance and the light follows.

There is a silence as my mother and I look out the window. I'm so glad that she was here with me to see all of this.

"You helped your father so much," she said.

Now, whenever I am in Madison, I think about what happened back then and as my mother gets older and I sit with her in that room, It's sad to look at that empty chair, and all the fond memories left behind.

Now she looks out that window. I just wonder what she is thinking about. I look down at the old Indian head penny in my hand. I smile to myself, I know what she is thinking, because I'm remembering the same person.

It doesn't matter where he is, "From Here To Heaven," we will always think of him.

#

The End

About the Author

Tom was born in 1947 in Madison, New Jersey. Although he no longer lives in Madison, he continues to hold his hometown close to his heart.

Shortly after his father's death, Tom made a promise that he would do everything possible to achieve what his father didn't in life. His desire was to know who his birth mother was.

After many years of searching, Tom accomplished this feat, but not without many obstacles.

In writing this emotional saga, Tom brings the past alive. He hopes that it will inspire others to remember their past and to search for their long lost loved-ones. For we all have a right to know where we came from.

Printed in the United States
6009